The Day They Kidnapped Queen Victoria

THE DAY
THEY KIDNAPPED
QUEEN VICTORIA

H.K. FLEMING

ST. MARTIN'S PRESS, NEW YORK

First published in the U.S.A. by St. Martin's Press 1978
Copyright © 1969 by H. K. Fleming
All rights reserved. For information, write:
St. Martin's Press, Inc., 175 Fifth Ave.,
New York, N.Y. 10010.
Manufactured in the United States of America

7.95

Library of Congress Cataloging in Publication Data

Fleming, Horace Kingston.
    The day they kidnapped Queen Victoria.

    1. Victoria, Queen of Great Britain, 1819-1901—
Fiction. I. Title.
PZ3.F6284Day 1978 [PS3511.L4417] 813'.5'4 77-15340
ISBN 0-312-18457-3

Dramatis Personae

Queen Victoria, *and her circle*:

Sir John Cowell, *Master of the Royal Household*
Colonel Henry Ponsonby, *Equerry*
General Grey, *Private Secretary*
Alfred Tennyson, *Poet Laureate*
Dr Jenner, *Physician*
Lady Ely, *Lady-in-waiting*
John Brown, *Attendant*
Emile Dittweiler, *Dresser*

Edward, Prince of Wales, *and his circle*:

Sir Francis Knollys, *Private Secretary*
Marquis of Hartington
Henry Chaplin
'Skittles' Walters

Benjamin Disraeli, Prime Minister, *and his circle*:

Monty Corry, *Private Secretary*
Lord Cairns, *Lord Chancellor*
Duke of Marlborough, *Lord President of the Council*
Lord Stanley, *Foreign Secretary*

Others:

Marquis of Hastings
Lady Hastings
Duke of Cambridge, *Field Marshal*
Edwin Landseer, *Painter*
Rev. Charles Anderson, *Vicar of St John's, Limehouse*
Earl of Kendal, *friend of the Prince of Wales*
Mary Nolan, *dresser to the Queen*

'Accordingly, on the night of 11 February 1867, the rebels in West Kerry rose. They captured a mounted orderly, sacked a coastguard station, and ultimately dispersed. The same evening, crowds of Irishmen began to assemble in Chester. They lounged about the city, and were gradually being recruited by comrades from the great centres of population in Lancashire. The fact was, a Fenian council in Liverpool had resolved to attack Chester Castle, and take possession of the arms which were known to be stored there. The railway rolling-stock was then to be secured, the telegraph wires cut, and trains of armed men run to Holyhead, where they were to seize all the steamers, proceed to Dublin, and continue the insurrection in Ireland.'

– from *The Reign of Queen Victoria*, edited by Humphrey Ward (Smith, Elder & Co, 1887)

I

As the Queen sat in her room at Balmoral Castle, she gazed at a blank page of her diary, heavily edged in mourning black. Seven years had passed since the death of her beloved Albert, and already scores of monuments, statues, and plaques, not to mention buildings and gardens – and one public convenience – had been dedicated to his name. But the ceremony to be held on the morrow was to be an especially poignant one.

She took a pen and wrote as follows:

'Tomorrow I am to visit the Duchess of Ayrshire at Ayrshire Castle to unveil a statue to my precious Albert in the castle grounds. The Duchess suggested that the date of the unveiling should coincide with the anniversary of my engagement to Albert, a most touching thought.

'For this occasion I have asked Bertie that he, too, be present so that he may honour his father's memory as, alas, he did not do when his father was alive.'[1]

A tear trickled down the Queen's cheek, and, impelled by some force that she was unable to resist, her fingers turned the pages to another date in her diary – 25th November. It was on that day seven years ago that her Albert, although weak and sick with fever, had felt compelled to travel to Cambridge to remonstrate with Bertie concerning his affair with a young actress. That journey had been his last. A fatal and fated journey, as the Queen believed, and in her mind the finger of fate pointed accusingly at her son. She composed her features with difficulty and now with thick lines scratched out the words: 'as, alas he did not do when his father was alive'. Some things were better left unsaid.

She continued writing: 'And I have most earnestly requested

1. Bertie = Edward, Prince of Wales.

that, in order to forestall any possible last-minute changes in his plans, Bertie's train from London be attached to mine, which I understand will be done at Stanley Junction.'

The Queen studied this sentence for a moment, then struck out the words 'I understand'. To herself she said, 'It *will* be done.'

These words were penned in the early morning while a Scotch mist still obscured the gorse and heather, and less than two hours later the Queen was driving away from Balmoral Castle. The road led to the small town of Ballater which among other things was the terminus of the Deeside Railway which ran to Aberdeen and there connected with the larger and more powerful Caledonian Railway. When the Queen arrived, the train was waiting and the engine puffing steam. A mass of flowers in window-boxes provided a flaming background, in contrast to the blue and green tartan of an officer of a Highland regiment, who was standing at attention.

The station-master, a Mr McCullogh, now began his final inspection. The handles of the train doors, he noted, were properly in the locked position. He saw the Queen sitting alone, her face a mask as usual, in the claret-coloured royal coach, built, as he well knew, in 1861, which was coupled next to the engine. Since the death of Albert, had she not always been alone? In this instance she was alone in a double sense, since there was no inside connection with the rest of the train, and the attendants could reach her only when the train stopped at a station; or, if there was no station, they had to make their way along the track and either clamber up or get hauled up by friendly hands.

It was a somewhat rustic coach for royalty, but a new one would not be ready until next year. There was a main compartment with a chair and table and a sofa, which, at night, became a bed. At one end was a bedroom and lavatory. At the other, rear, end was a separate tiny compartment for a sergeant-footman, with its own doors. Usually, on such trips his florid face was to be seen beaming from a window. This time he seemed to be snoozing ... Not like him at all.

In the second coach, which was, of course, divided into compartments, there was a mixture of court officials and attendants, actually only a handful. The Queen's lady-in-waiting, Lady Ely, occupied the first compartment, the two women dressers the second. In the third was the famous, not to say pugnacious, John Brown, the Queen's personal attendant, with his supply of tea and whisky. In the fourth sat the Queen's physician, Dr Jenner, along with her elderly Private Secretary, General Grey.

The third and last coach was used principally for luggage, but a valet and a couple of policemen sat there, along with the train guard. One other passenger completed the roster, but he was travelling on the footplate of the little engine. He was the general manager of the railway.

The station-master raised his hand; the guard waved a flag. The engine tooted as it clanked slowly out of the station in the direction of Aberdeen and the unseen and unsuspected future.

One of these who observed the departure of the royal train with emotions he rarely revealed to others, and then only to a very few, was Sir John Cowell, who held (for him) the improbable post of Master of the Royal Household. Somehow his career had led him down a strange path. He had a military background as did so many of those who were on the Queen's staff – Royal Engineers in his case. Then he had been selected for the delicate post of 'governor' to the royal children – the male version of governess, God save the mark; and in due course to 'governing' the Royal Household, where he found himself caught in a web of backstairs palace intrigues.

As he watched the train disappear round a bend, and the Queen with it, he was already thinking of Balmoral as a brighter place to live in. It was no longer a prison and almost approached being a hotel, although, of course, not of the first class. He breathed deeply. Freedom for a few days! Freedom from having even routine orders countermanded, and from receiving instructions, either in writing or by word of mouth, second and third and fourth hand, from ladies-in-waiting, governesses, cooks, and bottle-washers. He waved to the Highlander officer, Captain Leith, who happened to be a friend of his, and commanded a company of the 71st stationed near the castle. The two made their way to the station office, where McCullogh, the station-master, was already seated.

'How is the rest of the programme?' asked Sir John.

'Seems to be in hand, sir. Train left on time. Should arrive in Aberdeen on time and at Stanley Junction on time. There may be a short wait there until the Prince's train arrives from the south. Then the Prince's train will be attached . . . By the way, sir, I never heard of His Royal Highness's train being attached to Her Majesty's train before . . .' He coughed lightly. 'Not that there's any reason why not, of course . . .'

Sir John lit a large cigar, and puffed : a gesture of defiance that wasn't lost on his audience of two. The Queen detested tobacco and waged constant war on tobacco-smokers. 'No, no reason why not that I can see. Telegraph confirmation to me at Balmoral, will you? Captain Leith, I have a conveyance. Can I prevail on you to accompany me to the castle?' The Captain accepted, and the two men strode to the stable-yard of the Invercauld Arms, where one of the castle gigs was ready and waiting. With Sir John taking the reins, they were out in the country in a few minutes. The mist was lifting and the sun shone on a vista of larches, firs, gorse, thistle, heather, distant mountains, and low hills. The road led them north of the River Dee, but, on the south side, close to the river bank, they could see the other, parallel road and the slender thread of the telegraph-line that connected Balmoral Castle with the railroad station at Ballater.

For a while they drove in silence, which was broken by Sir John, who waved his whip in the direction of the telegraph-line. 'What continues to amaze me,' he said, 'is what has happened to us in the last thirty years; suddenly we have invisible communication. Then we have a new breed of men who understand the workings of such things, and, in a manner of speaking, live in a world of their own. They can talk with hundreds of others all over the country. Vast unseen network you might say.'

'Is personal chatter permitted?' asked the Captain.

'Officially, no. In practice it's impossible to stop it. You need as many monitors as operators. Whole thing too new anyway.' He gave his whip another wave in the direction of the telegraph wires and then stopped in mid-air with an exclamation. Subconsciously he pulled up the horse, which veered to the side of the road and came to a halt.

'Captain, your eyes are better than mine. Do you see what I'm pointing at?'

The Captain shielded his eyes. 'If you're pointing to the line, there isn't any.'

'But, of course there is.'

'Maybe there was,' said the Captain, who was peering intently up and down the river. 'But not now. There's several yards of line down, and that's a fact.'

Sir John stepped down from the trap, hitched the reins to a sapling and, followed by Leith, began striding through a meadow to the river bank to get a closer look. The Dee at this point swept across rocks and boulders, making music in its march to the sea, but no bridge, small boat, or stepping-stones were in sight. Now he could see that the wires were down.

In ten minutes they were back at Ballater station, making a return call on McCullogh, whom they found moodily eating an oatmeal and blood pudding. He heard them report their discovery without a change of expression, walked into an adjoining room where the telegraph instrument was, and tentatively tried it. There was silence as he wiped his face with an immense handkerchief. He shook his head. 'There seems to be no communication with Balmoral. The line is dead.' He made some adjustments and tried again, in fact several times. 'There is no communication the other way either.'

'What's that?' exclaimed Sir John. 'You mean the Aberdeen line is cut too?'

'Oh, I wouldn't know about cutting, Sir John. The wires do go down, you understand. Big trees and such. Sometimes the workmanship is at fault. It will all have to be carefully investigated.'

'Come now, how can both lines be down at the same time?'

McCullogh considered. 'No doubt a coincidence,' he said. He used his handkerchief again. 'Frankly, though, it's puzzling.'

'Damned puzzling,' spoke up the Captain. He began pacing the floor.

'And when was the telegraph to Aberdeen last used?' enquired Sir John.

'When Her Majesty's train departed.'

'And when was the telegraph to the castle last used?'

'Some time this morning.'

'How long will it take to make repairs?'

Sir John cut him short: 'McCullogh, I want a messenger to leave by road for Aberdeen within the next quarter-hour. Repairs must be made immediately. I want General Grey on the royal train informed. They can telegraph him a message out of Aberdeen ... Here, let me ...' He penned the following on a sheet of Deeside Railway note-paper:

'General Grey –

'Telegraph lines to Balmoral apparently cut in two places. No direct telegraphic communication available pending repairs. No immediate explanation. Investigating.

'Cowell'

The Master of the Household re-read it carefully, nodded, handed it to McCullogh.

'Now, Captain, Balmoral.'

Once back in the trap, Sir John kept the horse going at a fast pace, along the south road this time, and in a few minutes it needed only a glance to confirm their fears. Clearly the wire was cut and down.

There was something about the scene that inhibited conversation. Captain Leith's long lean face grew longer and leaner; he and his detachment of fifty men of the 71st Highland Regiment had responsibility for the protection of the Queen, not to mention the property of the Queen, although ordinary thefts and vandalism were properly police matters. But was this 'theft and vandalism' in any ordinary sense?

Sir John applied the whip, and in another thirty minutes they reached Balmoral Castle and were walking gloomy corridors.

The Captain rubbed his hands: 'Cold place, even colder than the barracks.'

14

'Yes, it's always cold here.'

'No fires?'

'Scarcely ever. Occasionally Her Majesty will permit them. We lead a Spartan life.'

Sir John turned into his office, which was as bleak as the rest of the place. Tartan wallpaper provided a backdrop for three uncomfortable chairs and an old desk. He closed a door, which creaked on monumental hinges.

'Sit down, Captain . . . And your opinion in a nut-shell?'

'Could be serious!'

'It could be. Yes. Yet inconclusive. Are we confronted with a coincidence, a crank, or a conspiracy?'

'What impresses me, Sir John, is the sequence. Two breaks in succession. For all we know there may be another break – after the train leaves Aberdeen . . .'

'We must admit the possibility. Then my message to General Grey would not get through. A message must be got through. What guarantee is there when repairs will be completed?'

They agreed to set up a temporary link – using a messenger relay – with some other telegraph system, and, since only the railway lines had the telegraph, the problem became one of geography and logistics. The map showed three or four possibilities, either over mountain trails, or through passes where a relay might operate.

There was no time to pick and choose, and they selected the cross-country route which led down Glen Tilt. It was the centre of a wild region where 10,000 deer roamed amid cascades, waterfalls, and streams. At the other end was the Highland Railway line and several railway stations – Glen Atholl, Killiecrankie, and so on. There were a few hunting-lodges and cottages *en route*. It was a forty-mile journey from the castle, and the job could be done by a combination of carriage, horse, and pony – the middle ten-mile section being a twisting, narrow stretch across the Grampian Mountains. Several years ago in the blissful heyday of her marriage, the Queen had undertaken that journey with Albert. The route had the strongest sentimental attraction for her.

15

'Who will you send?' asked Sir John.

'A sergeant and a squad of ten men,' replied Captain Leith. 'Two are telegraphists, by the way. I'd prefer to go with them myself, but I can't leave my post here.'

Sir John fingered the map. His post was at Balmoral, but only in a housekeeping sense. And he was sick of housekeeping. He needed fresh air and exercise, and to get away from the women. A small voice kept whispering to him: 'Captain Cowell of the Royal Engineers, you, too, are a telegraphist.'

What followed was inevitable. He volunteered to make the trip.

Captain Leith was surprised, then delighted. 'Wonderful,' he exclaimed. He jumped swiftly to his feet and walked to the barracks to collect his men.

While plans were being laid at Balmoral Castle, McCullogh, the station-master, was wasting no time in carrying out his instructions. He got as far as the Invercauld Arms with the intention of arranging for a post-boy to carry Cowell's message to Aberdeen, when he came to a decision which surprised him as much as it surprised the owner of the Arms, a Mrs Ross, when she heard of it. (A small voice kept whispering to McCullogh, as it had to Cowell. In his case, it seemed to be saying: 'McCullogh, you are a curious man, are you not? Do you not owe it to yourself to find out what devilment is going on here?')

He decided to go himself.

'*You*, going to Aberdeen *by road*, McCullogh, and paying for it, when your own Deeside Railway will take you there for nothing!' was the reaction of Mrs Ross. 'A gig costs fifteen shillings for the day, but in your case you can have it for twelve shillings and sixpence.'

'I want a gig as fast as possible, Mrs Ross, and for your information I'm not paying for it. Balmoral Castle will be paying for it. And, for your further information, I am carrying an important message concerning Her Majesty.'

'A grave matter of state, no doubt,' responded Mrs Ross, dryly. 'Well, Balmoral will have to pay the fifteen-shilling rate. They

16

can afford it.' She was about to shout instructions to the courtyard to set the ostler in motion when she halted and wiped her face thoughtfully with a bar cloth. 'What's all this to-do about, Mc-Cullogh?'

She was no fool, and McCullogh felt the need for someone to talk to . . . They were alone . . . He began haltingly and ended by telling all. She listened carefully and when she spoke she had a simple question :

'Might a pigeon do the trick?'

'I hadn't thought of it. A carrier pigeon ! Who has one?'

'My brother. He has a dozen of them. A mile down the road, as you know.'

'Quite an idea, Mrs Ross.' And why not? Pigeons had been carrying messages for centuries, and he had read somewhere that there had been a pigeon postal system in Baghdad in the year 1150, a piece of information he had regarded as completely useless – until now. The telegraph had been doing the job for only twenty or thirty years.

'Well, let's go and see him,' said Mrs Ross, who was a believer in direct action. In ten minutes they were in a gig, moving rapidly to Mrs Ross's brother, who, it turned out, kept bees and a couple of acres of vegetables, and lived in a low-slung stone cottage. The noise of buzzing merged with the mutterings of pigeons, doves, hens, and other birds perched on the fruit bushes.

He was a Highlander, and said very little, but he was a genuine pigeon-fancier. 'Certainly, my birds fly to Aberdeen all the time.'

All that remained were the details.

'And the man in Aberdeen will put it on the telegraph?'

'Certainly.'

'And what guarantee is there that it will get there?'

'None at all.'

McCullogh pondered. An idea came to him. In lieu of a guarantee, a certain amount of safety might be provided by spreading the field. He decided to duplicate the message.

As an old soldier, with the Highland Brigade, he felt an affinity to those who had been with him in the Crimea. His commander had been the Duke of Cambridge, cousin of Her Majesty, now promoted to the highest rank – Field Marshal and Commander-in-Chief. The Duke had once said a cheery word to him on the battlefield: it would never be forgotten. A picture of the Duke hung in the waiting-room at Ballater station, flanking one of the Queen.

The Duke in London would receive a copy along with General Grey.

2

Colonel Ponsonby, Equerry to the Queen, was not accompanying her on her trip to Ayrshire Castle because the Almighty had intervened. An uncle of his had died in London. He had approached Her Majesty for a brief leave from Balmoral and she had consented, with reluctance. While she was deeply sympathetic to bereavement – she herself had now become almost a professional mourner – she also looked with distaste on anything that might cause her the slightest inconvenience.

While in London, the Colonel had decided to undertake two confidential missions, but he had mentioned neither of them to the Queen. The first he was undertaking now. He was pacing slowly up a platform at Euston station, a commanding yet oddly professional figure, in baggy civilian clothes. In a manner of speaking, he was there to pay respects to the Prince of Wales upon his departure for the north to attend the unveiling. But he was also there out of caution, curiosity, and some inner concern. All was not well between the Queen and the Prince.

The scene confronting him was familiar. Footmen in livery were scurrying about. He noted the refined fittings on the Prince's new coach. It was built of teak, twenty-seven feet long, coloured blue and white. It was much superior to the Queen's, but this was to be expected. It was larger and had no less than four compartments – two saloons and two 'retiring rooms', in which sofas pulled out to form sleeping couches. Even the luggage glittered . . . A picture floated through his mind of the dowdy lady in far-away Balmoral and the values she stood for: and here was the opposite side of the coin – for whatever moral might be drawn from it. His musings were interrupted by a tap on the shoulder: it was the Prince himself, and it was clear he was not in a jovial mood. With him was his equerry, Sir Francis Knollys, with whom Ponsonby was on friendly terms; in fact, between the two of them, the equerries several times had been able to divert royal collisions.

'Ponsonby!'

'Good morning, sir.'

'Ponsonby, what do you know about these train arrangements?'

'Not much, sir.'

'This business of attaching my train to the Queen's – what is the point of it? What is the reason for it?'

'I really can't speak for Her Majesty, sir.'

'Well, you must have *some* views. What are they?'

'May I speak frankly, sir?'

'Certainly; I expect it.'

'Your mother has a deep attachment to Ayrshire. I believe it was there your father first hunted.'

'Was it? I probably wasn't born at the time.'

'Yes, sir, and your father's portrait was painted there several times. By Landseer. In hunting costume. With stags.'

'So!' The Prince had a wonderfully musical voice when he cared to turn on the charm; but he was not half German for nothing, and the 'So!' was a guttural one.

'Your Royal Highness, your mother feels strongly about this particular ceremony. Just as she has deep feelings for you, sir. And I am sure that what she had in mind was that family unity be symbolized.'

The Prince's expression mirrored mixed emotions for an instant. He had never had a normal childhood, and he had built up a façade . . . He blinked and walked away.

Knollys, who remained, waited until he was out of ear-shot. He whispered: 'Ponsonby, old man – the real story?'

'She is forcing him to the penitential seat, of course.'

'So I suspected,' said Knollys. 'We've our work cut out for

us. HRH has quite an affair planned for himself and his friends in the Highlands; this is seriously going to interrupt it . . . According to my accounting, this is the seventh unveiling of an Albert monument in the last three years. Filial duty is a fine thing, but there's a limit somewhere . . .' He shook his head and turned to watch a small shunting-engine bring up two more coaches evidently to be added to the rear of the train. With some surprise, Ponsonby observed that they were both private, elegant, and both adorned with coats of arms; and at that moment two dissimilar figures emerged from a station door, surrounded by a small army of porters and valets.

No one who knew anything about Society (with a capital S) needed to ask who they were. One was the Marquis of Harting-ton, who looked like a tramp, and would one day be the eighth Duke of Devonshire, and whose mistresses were legion. The other was the monocled Henry Chaplin, one of the wildest spenders in the kingdom, and owner of a string of racehorses. For a brief moment he halted, as a messenger held out to him what seemed to be an envelope. After a fleeting glance at it, he put it in his pocket. These were the Prince's cronies.

Ponsonby felt a prickly sensation down his spine. 'Knollys, are they on this train?' he asked.

'Quite so.'

'Is it wise, on this occasion?'

'My dear fellow, I follow orders, and survive by not asking too many questions. The Queen wanted the trains combined. I don't recall she said anything about any guests the Prince might have on his end of the combination . . .'

Further conversation was cut short by a guard's whistle, discreet and tentative, befitting the impending departure of Great Personages. Knollys glided away.

The Prince was already in his coach, and apparently, for a part of the journey at least, his cronies were to be with him. They were there too. The Marquis of Hartington, however, kept peer-ing down the platform. Someone was expected.

There was a stir among a group of porters at the far end and a slim young woman, tastefully dressed, came into view. Hartington waved lazily. She walked to him and the royal coach door closed behind her. The train puffed its way out of Euston station. Ponsonby walked off the platform with a sense of foreboding. Once outside, he hailed a cab, and, after consulting a notebook, directed the cabbie, in a double-breasted yellow raincoat, to No 1 St John's Wood Road. He was bound on his second mission. The face of the girl on the train seemed vaguely familiar. Or was it? He closed his eyes, and, leaning back against the seat, reviewed the faces he had seen at dinners, receptions, teas, and parties. He could evoke no clue; the answer must lie elsewhere, and that was what he was afraid of. 'Elsewhere' could be dangerous, even treacherous, territory. The cabbie was taking the direct route along Euston Road, skirting Regent's Park, into Park Road; Ponsonby found himself at his destination sooner than he expected. He alighted, told the cabbie to wait, and pulled a doorbell. A small brass plaque bore the words 'SIR EDWIN LANDSEER'.

A maid admitted him and escorted him into a huge studio, bright with light from two doors which opened on to a garden shaded by mulberry trees. The artist himself was missing – until Ponsonby spotted him about twenty yards away. But was that really he? An elderly figure was on hands and knees, peering through the palings of a fence at a massive dog. The dog, surprised, to use no stronger term, at the apparition that evidently had interrupted his afternoon stroll, was beginning to make low growling noises, shifting by degrees from neutral to hostile, when Landseer, to the dog's even greater surprise, began making growling noises of his own.

Suddenly he gave vent to a snarl that was alarming in its realism; the dog tottered back and raced madly off into the distance.

It was the maid who said the next word, with a strong Welsh accent – she too had been watching: 'Sometimes the master gives a wrong impression. There are those who could think he's barmy.' Ponsonby felt it wise to remain non-committal.

'And that's just what some do think,' continued the maid. 'But it isn't so. His mind may be a bit wobbly now and again.

But he's as wonderful at imitating the cries of animals as he is at painting animals, and he's done it all his life. Now and again he likes to try hisself out to see if he's lost his touch. Ask that dog what he thinks. He will say the old man has got a better flow of language than he has . . .' She retired, presumably to the kitchen. The painter was now coming across the garden, a burly figure with white hair and a broad, frank face, and Ponsonby began to recall the stories he had heard about him from the Queen as well as from Albert. He had been a favourite of both of them for a quarter of a century. As an artist, he had been their type – sentimental and inclined to gloominess. More: he had taught them both to draw. He had been an artistic prodigy as a child, and he could work equally with his right or left hand.

'Colonel Ponsonby, how nice to see you again. The last time . . . ah, that was quite a few years ago . . .'

'It was indeed, Sir Edwin. Ayrshire Castle.'

'Of course.' It is doubtful if he really recalled the place. About seven years ago, his reason had clouded over – some said it was on account of his sensitivity at imagined personal slights. He had not painted since, but now, miraculously, he was recovering.

Ponsonby charted a careful conversational course and then gradually led into his mission . . . 'One painting you did at Ayrshire, Sir Edwin, interests me particularly. And it would be of great interest to the Queen.'

'Would be? Wasn't it finished?'

'No.'

'What one was that?'

'A happy group at the time, the happiest, the Queen, the Prince Consort, and the Prince . . . Could you be prevailed upon to finish it?'

Lines of doubt furrowed the painter's brow; he stroked his moustache. 'I'm trying to recall. Something broke a spell there.' Ponsonby watched him without seeming to. It was this picture that marked a milestone in his decline: it marked the beginning of it. Completion would signal recovery and victory.

'You say the Queen would be gratified?' asked Landseer.

'Sir Edwin, this particular picture would have a deep effect on her.' He spoke with conviction. Anything that recalled for the Queen happy days with Albert had to be a success, and the Prince would benefit through association. Landseer walked to the far end of the studio and began shuffling canvasses which were stacked in piles. At last he found what he was looking for. More than half finished. He studied it intently. Ponsonby joined him, then left him to his meditations and turned to look at other canvasses: deer, stags, otters, sheep – animals of the farm and field, with the subdued Landseer touch, that had raised sales prices to huge figures. There were so many of them around that his eye was caught by the unexpected colours of a costume painting, half concealed in a corner. He saw that it was a preliminary sketch, and no doubt someone had the original. It was 'The Taming of the Shrew'.

As Ponsonby recalled it later, the silence in the room seemed to become oppressive, as he was immersed at one end and Sir Edwin at the other, each lost in his own thoughts. It took Ponsonby a few seconds to focus properly . . . and then there wasn't any doubt about it. The girl with the grey-blue eyes and brown hair he had seen on the railway platform, who had walked into the Prince's coach, was now confronting him as a character out of Shakespeare. She was Katharina, of Padua, the shrew; Landseer had used her as a model. There was no room for error. He walked across the room with his finger pointed at her, and hesitantly approached the painter.

'Eh . . . what's that?' Sir Edwin found it hard to cope with a rapid change of subject. 'That was an Academy picture.' He pulled a bell and the maid reappeared. 'Myfanwy, your memory is better than mine. Do you recall that model?'

Myfanwy peered and grinned wickedly. 'We told everyone that was Miss Gilbert. But it wasn't.'

'Well, who was it?'

'Skittles.'

'Skittles? . . . Skittles?'

'Skittles Walters. She lived down the road, at the small yellow house, with another girl. Oh, she had some influential friends, she did, a carriage and horses too. How did she get them? A nice question.' She sniggered. 'Or perhaps a nasty question.'

'I'm beginning to remember,' said Landseer. 'Colonel Ponsonby, I think it better not to dwell on this. If you don't mind.'

'Quite understandable,' replied the Colonel. He had heard all he wanted anyway.

Ponsonby was walking to his cab round the corner when he spotted a carriage with a liveried coachman. As he passed by, he saw a coat of arms, and a glance was enough (for him) to tell the owner. The Marquis of Hastings was in the neighbourhood; to his astonishment he saw that it was at the small yellow house. When he reached his cab he sat down to think. He felt a responsibility to find out more about Skittles Walters, if he could, but his training hadn't fitted him for the role of detective. He also had to be infinitely cautious; he moved in high places. He communed regularly with the Queen, with the Royal Dukes, with other Dukes, with Mr Disraeli, with members of the cabinet; he was privy to state secrets. Could he become a spy in St John's Wood (of all places), home of artists, actresses and the *demimondaines*? Dare he become involved?

The answer was: yes. The presence of the Marquis decided him. But how long was the Marquis going to stay around? No sooner had he posed the question than he got the answer. The Marquis came out, with a silk hat tilted rakishly on his head, cane in hand. The carriage drove off.

Ponsonby waited ten minutes, then walked up the trim path and pulled the bell. A young woman with blonde hair answered.

She blurted out an unexpected question, 'The police?'

'No, I am not the police. Why should I be?'

'What do you want?'

'I am looking for a young lady I understand lived here. The name is Walters.'

A look of relief seemed to pass over the girl's face – or was he mistaken? Yet suspicion remained. 'Skittles Walters? Everyone knows where she lives.'

'I don't. Perhaps I lead too sheltered a life.'

'And why should I tell you about Skittles?'

'Look, young lady, I'm not going to eat you.' And she saw

that he wasn't. He had a kind face. Clothes good, but quite old-fashioned.

She brushed back a stray hair. 'I'm sorry. Come in if you'd care to.' He entered a room filled with knick-knacks and with a parrot muttering in a corner. In a post of honour on the wall was an engraved reproduction of 'The Taming of the Shrew'.

She invited him to sit down, adding, 'I didn't get the name.'

'I didn't give any.'

'Incognito, is it? Well, that doesn't worry me. Too many gentlemen do the same. My name is Cora Duke.'

'Why did you think I was the police?' asked Ponsonby. 'Do I look like a policeman?'

'Now I see you, no . . .'

'Did the Marquis travel incognito?' He was surprised at the effect of this question. First, what looked like a tear, then cynicism.

She blurted out : 'Do you know him?'

'I know about him.'

'How much do you know?'

'I'm old enough to be discreet.'

She shrugged her shoulders. 'Well, I'm not. The Marquis is ill. He is worse off than he thinks. Do you know Mott's in Foley Street?'

'I can't say that I do.'

'I didn't think you did. You aren't the type. Call it a dance hall, with added attractions. The Marquis had his little joke there last night. He let two hundred loose rats out of sacks on the ballroom floor. At least, one of his men let 'em loose.'

Ponsonby whistled. 'What happened?'

'You can guess. People got hurt and got bit.'

'What happened to Hastings?'

'Nothing, of course.'

'You sure about all this?'

'I was there.'

'How long have you known him?'

'Two years.'

'And you put up with him?'

Her look, her shrug, and her silence were eloquent.

She walked to a dresser where she produced a decanter of sherry and a couple of wine-glasses. Without asking him she poured twice. She began talking quickly ... 'You wonder why I'm telling you this? You happen to be here at the right time, that's why ... You look like you could be trusted, and I'm not used to that ... And I've half an idea I've seen you before somewhere. Would Hastings know you if he saw you?'

Ponsonby nodded. 'Probably.'

'And what's your interest in Skittles?'

'Information. Nothing more. She'll not be harmed.'

'Harmed!' Cora shook her head. 'Harmed by who? She's under the protection of some of the highest in the land. She has two thousand a year, a house in Mayfair, a carriage, horses, a groom, and other servants. All from Hartington.'

There was a muttering from the parrot's cage. The bird cackled, 'Harty-Tarty!'

'And poets write poems about her,' continued Cora. 'She's done better than any of us. Top of the profession, you might say.' She drank to the health of Skittles. 'She has Hartington: I *had* Hastings!'

Ponsonby held his sherry up to what little light was filtering through the lace curtains.

He mused aloud. 'I saw Skittles, I think, this morning. At Euston station.'

'No!' exclaimed Cora.

'Yes, why not?'

'Was she on a train?'

'She did get on a train.'

'*His* train – the Prince's?'

Ponsonby nodded. The girl had become quite agitated. Finally she exclaimed, 'That does it, then.'

'Does what?'

'I've got to talk to someone, and there's no time to waste.'

'Who do you mean by someone?'

'Someone who can do something. Who can act – now ... No, don't tell me to go to the police ...'

All Ponsonby could think of to say was, 'I may be able to help you, if you'll let me.' That proved to be enough. Cora gave him a searching look.

'Very well,' she said. 'Hastings is planning another of his jokes. He's aiming higher. It's got something to do with the Prince's train.'

Ponsonby felt a chill. 'Does he know that the Prince's train is going to be attached to the Queen's train?'

'Is it? ... No, I don't know ... I doubt if he'd care.'

'What is the joke?'

She shook her head. 'He wouldn't tell me. But I'm sure his coachman knows. He was at Mott's last night. I think he'll be there tonight.'

'Will he talk?'

'I think he's ready. He's had enough.'

'I should like to meet him,' said Ponsonby, and the rest seemed to follow inevitably. His involvement was becoming total. The girl wasted little time putting on a coat and hat, and they were on their way, sitting side by side in the cab, to Foley Street. He was relieved to see that she was a quiet dresser. The steady clop-clop of the horse's hooves encouraged reflection ... The Prince also had been going to Mott's, Ponsonby knew. He knew, too, from the correspondence which he handled, that a storm was arising in the country about the Prince's conduct: all that was needed to create a whirlwind was the revelation that the Queen of Courtesans was in the Prince's party, *en route* to a rendezvous with the unsuspecting Queen of England. And on a sacred occasion!

He shuddered.

They came to Mott's as twilight began to envelop London. Without hesitating, she took him through an octagonal ballroom. Porters were still scrubbing bloodstains off the floor and some dead rats were piled in baskets. There was a smell of distant cooking and stale perfumes. Three tired musicians were beginning to tune up for the night's dancing. The crowd hadn't begun to arrive yet, but already girls were scattered about the gaming-rooms, bar-rooms, private rooms. Although Cora walked by them, within arm's length, they ignored her : she moved in circles that were beyond them. Ponsonby followed, a shadow in his sombre clothes. He was being noted, of course. The men who kept watch in doorways raised their eyebrows : no more was necessary.

Now Ponsonby and the girl were moving along a second-floor corridor. 'Joe ought to be around here,' she said. And he was, a scrawny figure with a seamed face, almost enveloped in his coachman's hat. His whip lay on the table in front of him, beside a filled tankard and two unfilled ones. He was in what seemed to be some sort of anteroom.

'Joe, this gentleman would like to see you.'

'Well, and so he can, me dear. Who is he?' ... ('Looks like a bloody undertaker,' he added under his breath.)

Ponsonby sat down slowly alongside Cora, and, as he did so, he caught sight of the figure of a waiter, sidling from a recess. It seemed familiar : bushy head, wild beard, broken spectacles. The figure almost completed an exit when it reversed itself, and Ponsonby realized who it was – O'Toole, recently a telegraphist at Windsor Castle. O'Toole had just been dismissed, on the direct order of the Queen, because of a garbled message. Ponsonby had done what he could to save him, but it had been impossible.

O'Toole gave a grin that was a grimace and showed a lot of broken teeth. 'Most unexpected, Colonel. I never thought to see Her Majesty's equerry in this place.'

'I'm quite surprised myself.'

'Her Majesty's health is good, I presume.'

'Excellent, thank you.'

'Let us be thankful,' said O'Toole, with mock piety. 'The thoughts of all the O'Tooles remain with her – as you can understand ...' He disappeared.

The other three sat digesting the exchange. In fifteen seconds, word had reached the manager in a back room that upstairs was the Queen's own equerry, and, within forty-five seconds, the manager was overseeing the laying of a cloth (by another waiter), also of a cold beef and kidney pie and several bottles.

'I don't recall ordering any of this,' hazarded Ponsonby.

'Courtesy of the management,' was the response. 'Understand

you are new to the premises, sir. You might call this an introduction. Advertising. We cater to the nobility, as you are doubtless aware ... Ha, ha, who knows but that one day Her Majesty in person may be tripping the light fantastic here. No offence, sir. Easy come; easy go. We live for today. One big, happy family, as you might say ...'

I'm getting in deeper and deeper in all directions, thought Ponsonby. Cora cut him a large piece of pie and he began to eat. Joe was already exploring one of the bottles.

He made one digression, however – on the subject of rats.

'There's a wonderful deal of difference in rats,' mused Joe. 'The water- and sewer-rats lives on filth, but your barn rat is a plump fellow and he lives on the best of everything. He's well off. There's as much difference between the barn- and the sewer-rats as between a brewer's horse and a costermonger's.

'A rat's bite is very singular; it's a three-cornered one, like a leech's only deeper, and the best cure I ever found for it was the thick bottom of porter casks put on as a poultice. These porter bottoms is so powerful and draws so, they'll actually take the thorns out of horses' hooves after steeplechasing ...'

He continued. 'Those that was let out here was sewer rats'; and with this contribution he took a long drink and lapsed into silence.

An orchestra started up downstairs. The evening was young, and it would be some hours before merriment would take over; it might also, as Ponsonby feared, be some hours before he disentangled sense from nonsense. Or vice versa.

3

The Prince's train sped northward. His Royal Highness looked content – and why not? A couple of bottles of champagne were already open. A valet was busy with a stupendous hamper and was putting the contents on a side-table. A glance revealed cold partridges, smoked oysters and various items under glass, as well as ham and venison ... and this was only a beginning. Lord Hartington looked exactly as he would on any occasion, because, as his friends said, he had only one expression : indifference. Skittles looked bright and attentive, and was humming a tune to herself, while she watched the Prince open his celebrated card-case. It was well filled – baccarat chips with the royal monogram, and packs of cards, also monogrammed, He was smoking a big cigar while he handled the cards with his chubby fingers. Now and again he smiled at her fondly.

'What are you humming, Skitsie?'

'Nothing new, sir. Just an old one.'

'Let's hear it.' That was a command, of course, as she well knew. She started with a low but clear voice. Hartington himself had paid for her music lessons.

> 'Alas! my love, you do me wrong
> To cast me off discourteously,
> And I have lovéd you so long,
> Delighting in your company.
> For Greensleeves was all my joy,
> O Greensleeves was my delight,
> And Greensleeves was my heart of gold,
> And who but my Lady Greensleeves?'

The Prince laughed, then stopped suddenly. He glanced covertly at Chaplin, the remaining member of his party, who was reclining in a chair, with his monocle in his eye. He was gazing at the fleeting scenery, and in one hand he held a piece of paper, in fact the letter which had been handed to him at Euston station. Skittles clapped her hand to her forehead, as one who has made a gaffe. She gave the Prince a look of childlike guilt. Henry Chaplin had, in real life, been cast off discourteously. His bride-to-be, fresh from trying on the wedding-dress, had run off with another man – and the man was the Marquis of Hastings.

Chaplin turned round in his chair. He saw the Prince and Skittles watching him as though they shared a secret, but he had been so absorbed in his own thoughts that he had heard only a muted noise in the background while Skittles was singing. A curious expression on his face caused the Prince to ask: 'What's the matter, Harry?'

'Bit embarrassing, sir.'

'Too much so to let us in on the secret?'

'Really, I don't quite know how to take it. I was given this letter on the platform ... It's from Florence ...'

'Ah!' The Prince's voice was guttural when he felt emotion – which was frequently. Here was a coincidence, if it could be called such. In any event, his capacity for enjoying gossip was unlimited, and here was gossip directly from the source.

Florence was the wayward fiancée – once Lady Paget, but now, of course, Lady Hastings. He had a personal interest in the affair. Henry Chaplin (but called Harry) was one of his really close friends. He had been at Oxford with him, and he had ridden his horses there. A stable of them was always on hand. He had been looking forward to attending the Chaplin wedding, and the news of the denouement had stunned him as it had everyone else. Even the details of the affair taxed credulity. It had been established that Florence had gone to make some last-minute purchases at Marshall and Snelgrove's in Oxford Street, and there, obviously by arrangement, had been met by Hastings. What followed was not a shopping expedition, but a runaway morning marriage ceremony at St George's Church. It was a society sensation of the first water, yet Chaplin, true to his code, had maintained a stiff upper lip.

The Prince exchanged a quick glance with Skitsie. No! Verses about being done wrong and being cut off discourteously were *not* in order.

'You might call this a warning, sir,' continued Chaplin, who was concerned solely with the letter in his hand. He adjusted his monocle. 'Perhaps I had better read it:

'Dear Harry,

'This is a most difficult letter to write as you may well imagine. I suppose it is no secret to you, as well as others, that Henry is in desperate bad health as well as seriously in debt. I am afraid his conduct is quite unpredictable. For some reason, Harry, he has had a feeling, or should I say obsession, that he must challenge or humiliate you for reasons that are beyond me, but which I can only put down to his illness. We must face the possibility that his brain may be affected. What an irony, Harry, when I deserted you so shamefully.

'I am betraying a trust, I suppose, when I tell you that he has some sort of plan in mind to inconvenience you on your trip to Scotland with the Prince. I have to use the word "inconvenience" because I have no knowledge of the details, and what he has in mind could be something silly and foolish or quite awkward, even serious. I wouldn't put anything past him at this time, so please do be careful.'

The Prince listened gravely. 'I'll be damn'd' was his first reaction. 'What has he got against *you* after what he has done! I can see what *you* have got against him.'

Chaplin shook his head.

'I'm baffled.'

'I keep thinking of Hermit, sir,' continued Chaplin.

They all began to think of Hermit. Hermit was Chaplin's horse which had won the Derby. The horse had broken a blood vessel and had been withdrawn, but later the injury was found to be superficial. Chaplin re-entered him and he won. In the meantime, Hastings had been betting against Hermit like a man possessed and when the blow fell he had lost not less than £120,000. He was said to be on the road to ruin, and already had had to sell one of his huge estates. Strange hates and rivalries were evident here.

'Well, what do we do?' demanded the Prince irritably. 'If Hastings is after our Harry, we may all be on the firing-line.' A fearsome thought struck him. 'Including the Queen.'

'Harry ought to alert the palace – Ponsonby – as soon as possible,' suggested Hartington. 'He can telegraph him from the next station, wherever that is. The railway people should be alerted . . .'

'Hastings ought to be under guard,' the Prince snorted. 'Let's bring in Knollys – he's going to have to handle this.'

He bellowed at the valet: 'Pull the alarm cord! Stop the dam' train!' The valet pulled; the train came to a grinding stop that shot the cards off the table. They were in low-lying country. Just a few yards away was a canal, and meandering along it was a barge pulled by a horse, and aided by a small brown sail. The bargee and his fat wife were sprawled out on the deck, taking in the scene. They had no way of knowing that they were viewing history in the making.

Knollys, who was asleep, was rudely awakened. He peered out of the window of his coach, and saw a guard and a porter running down the tracks. Curious, and even alarmed, he clambered down himself, when he caught sight of the Prince waving to him. He hoisted himself up and joined the royal party.

The train restarted, leaving the barge behind . . . The council of war began immediately.

At 7.30 that evening, with blinds drawn, the Prince's train arrived at Kendal Junction. The station oil-lamps were dim, and the grey stones of the north country made the place look cold. The Earl of Kendal, known to the Prince and his two companions since their Oxford days as 'Porky' – on account of his tubby shape – was waiting for them on the platform. He was to be their host for a brief stay overnight. Alongside him was his wife; an old friend of the Prince, she had joined him at many an after-theatre champagne-party, when she was known as that adorable actress Muriel LeClerq. Both Earl and Countess boarded the Prince's coach for greetings.

One attraction of Kendal Castle as a stopping-place was that a spur railway led directly to it, affording privacy; the Earl owned altogether some fifty miles of railway. There were no mayors or aldermen anywhere around, and no journalists. There was nothing the Prince wanted less than the attention of the Press.

The engine that had pulled them from London was unhitched, and Knollys stood by in the evening air to watch it and to pass on a ten-pound note to the driver – a token from HRH. As he watched the new engine being backed in, a smaller but grander version, carrying the Kendal coat of arms, he realized that the Earl, who had just joined him, was personally going to drive it. He was putting on heavy gloves and a workman's hat.

'Knollys,' said the Earl, 'join me, will you? I want some advice.' Knollys clambered up on to the footplate. The Earl took the controls. The driving-wheel slipped a couple of times, then took hold, and they were off, slowly. The line led for some six miles through fields, across streams. Deer, pheasant, and partridge seemed to be everywhere.

'Tell you what the problem is, old fellow,' said the Earl, keeping his eye on the rails ahead. 'We've got a guest that HRH doesn't know about. Since this is his own private party, so to speak, how do you think he'll take to it?'

'Who is the guest?'

'Alfred Tennyson, the poet.'

Knollys considered this news as the train took a sharp curve and he had to hang on to an iron bar. When matters of social intercourse were involved, or questions of etiquette, the Prince could react violently. 'What happened,' continued the Earl, 'is that I've become a bit of an expert on King Arthur and the Round Table. The Holy Grail and that sort of thing. Surprising all right. Doesn't mix with railways at all. Anyway, it's just the subject Tennyson writes about ... Heard he was in the neighbourhood, and, dash it, I had to invite him ...'

'Where is he now?' asked Knollys.

'He has quarters of his own – the west wing. Poets like privacy, or so I was told.'

'Good. Keep him there until I can check the lie of the land. Now I've got a question. I've got to have the use of a telegraph.'

'We can manage that. There's a railway station at the castle, and a telegraph there. May have to fish the operator out of the local pub, though.'

They arrived at what turned out to be a miniature station, built in the Gothic style. Doors opened; the train disgorged its passengers; faces that had been hidden showed themselves. Attending His Royal Highness were two valets, a personal footman, and two porters. Hartington and Chaplin had a valet apiece. Skittles had a maid, an elderly lady who had been the wife of a Welsh Baptist minister (until he decamped) and spoke with a strong accent. It was an animated scene. Above, the castle battlements, five hundred years old. Below, the red glow issuing from the engine fire-box; the throng on the platform, and a medley of bats flying in and out of the shadows.

The party moved inside and were shown to their quarters.

Half an hour elapsed before Knollys could get the ear of the Prince, whom he found walking with Skittles along a corridor dotted with suits of armour. He broke the news about Tennyson.

'A bloody poet,' exclaimed the Prince. 'After a day's trip! And we have to be up in the morning at some God-forsaken hour. Porky must be out of his mind.'

A silence followed. Skittles started to say something, but didn't.

'Well, speak up, speak up.'

'I have to admit being partial to poets, sir.'

'Why? What do *you* know about them?'

'Someone wrote a poem about me once.'

'Ha! I don't believe it. What was it?'

'I'll only give you one verse, sir.

'Who might describe the humour of that night,
The mirth, the tragedy, the grave surprise,
The treasures of fair fclly, infinite
Learned as a lesson from those childlike eyes.'

The Prince was decidedly taken aback. This verse had genuine taste and feeling. Someone had a romantic vision of Skittles, and it was certain that Hartington couldn't put anything together like that. He doubted if Skittles knew how good it was.

'Who was the author?' he asked. 'No, don't tell me if you don't want to.'

Skittles furrowed her brow. 'I'll tell *you*, and I'll whisper it. His name was Blunt.'

'Blunt?'

'Must be Wilfred Scawen Blunt,' put in Knollys. 'How did you know he wrote it about you?'

Skittles smiled. '*I* know.'

'Well, what do we do about Tennyson?' pressed Knollys.

'Oh, go ahead,' said the Prince. 'Tell Porky to do what he wants.'

Skittles clapped her hands. 'Thank you, sir.'

'Always asking, asking, asking,' mumbled the Prince, but not really meaning it.

So the way was cleared. The butler sounded a great gong, the call for dinner. The guests assembled. The Poet Laureate appeared

35

and bowed low to the Prince. He was a giant of a man who ambled rather than walked. The leonine head, the imposing beard – here was no simpering versifier. The Prince began to feel that the evening might be salvaged after all. He squeezed the arm of Lady Kendal, his escort, as they began moving into dinner.

Tennyson was the partner of Skittles. He was near-sighted and he had to peer at her closely; and what he saw was what others saw, at first glance: big blue-grey eyes, chestnut hair, ingenuous mouth, slim hands. The poet began to murmur some lines to himself, but as he was absent-minded and had a voice like an organ, they were not the secret he supposed:

> 'Elaine the fair, Elaine the lovable,
> Elaine, the lily maid of Astolat,
> High in her chamber up a tower to the east
> Guarded the sacred shield of Lancelot...'

He paused, as if turning something over in his mind. He said suddenly, 'Your stays are creaking.'

Skittles gave a start and then burst out laughing. 'Not my stays, sir,' she said, demurely. 'Your braces, I think.'

'What's that? What's that?' exclaimed Tennyson, who in some ways was as direct and childlike as his partner.

'What I told you,' said Skittles.

'I believe you're right,' chuckled Tennyson. 'Tell me, who are you? Where do you fit in here?'

'Just a friend.'

The subject dropped. They were moving into the dining-hall. The table was ablaze with candles. Behind every chair stood a footman in the Kendal livery, except for the Prince's footman who had travelled with him from London. A butler hovered in the background.

Tennyson shook his head. 'Don't like it. Don't like it.'

'Don't like what?' enquired Skittles, as they took their places and settled themselves.

'Footmen,' breathed Tennyson, in a hoarse whisper, at the same time glancing uneasily over his shoulder. 'Being waited on.'

The Prince had overheard these odd interchanges, and was growing more amiable by the minute. In addition, the flame that always smouldered within him was being relit by his nearness to Lady Kendal. 'And how do you propose to order things otherwise, Mr Tennyson?' he asked.

'I can only speak for myself, sir,' growled the poet. 'They intimidate me; I feel I am being watched. Where is privacy? I prefer the hostess to do the serving. Pass it around. Or let everyone help themselves.'

'Come off it, Mr Tennyson,' said Lady Kendal, reverting for a moment to the days when she lived in a theatre boarding-house in Brixton. 'Privacy at a dinner-party! What are you talking about? You expect me to be hostess and handle all the plates too? And we have to be practical – how far away do you think the kitchen is in this place? It must be all of seventy-five yards.'

'That's the logic of it,' admitted Tennyson. 'I never could stand up against logic. I once used the phrase "the ringing grooves of change" in referring to railways. Then I found out that trains don't run in grooves; they run on raised rails. That comes of being short-sighted and looking inward for the image; your poet is a recluse, and I fear he rarely cuts much of a figure in society.'

'The way to cut a figure in society is to be yourself,' observed the Prince. 'You have no need to worry, Mr Tennyson. Tell me, what led you to concern yourself with King Arthur?'

'I immersed myself in the legends, sir. Then I came to see him as a sort of Voice of Conscience. I could quote *ad infinitum*, but there's a place and time for everything.' He thought it best to leave it at that. His intuition told him that the Prince had no interest at all in a serious discussion.

The Prince smiled. He thought: There's a rough honesty here; says what he means; doesn't talk too much. As he sipped his champagne, he recalled that his father had had the highest opinion of the poet, had visited him at his home, and had been deeply impressed by one poem in particular – *In Memoriam*. A gloomy job as the Prince remembered it. Written for some close friend. But his father and his mother read it endlessly. They read it together and read it alone.

When his father died, the palace copy of *In Memoriam* became sacred. Not only did his mother revere it as an object that had been touched by *him*, but in her own mind she came somehow to believe that the exalted sentiments had been written about *him*, her dear Albert, in the first place.

What with one thing and another, Tennyson, in the Queen's eye, stood above ordinary men. The bond was a mystic one that no one else could approach or share.

The germ of an idea had been emerging as this chain of thought unfolded, and the Prince put it into words:

'Mr Tennyson, I wonder if it would be convenient for you to accompany me tomorrow ...?' and he outlined the details of the ceremony to be held at Ayrshire Castle. Tennyson was taken aback, flattered. He decided to accept the invitation, and the Prince's train now would leave with an additional passenger aboard. Tennyson – representing one way of life – would accompany Skittles – representing another.

You take the high road; I'll take the low road – and we'll be in Scotland together.

Ponsonby left Mott's at 9.30 p.m. and put Cora in a cab for her home. He was not a type she had met before; she was intrigued, and she was reluctant to leave him, and she was available.

Ponsonby was not available. He hailed a hansom and told the driver to get him to Buckingham Palace as fast as possible.

'*Buckingham* Palace, guv'nor?'

'That's what I said.'

'I've been hacking in this city for well nigh forty years, and never had a passenger ask for any palace until you came along. A red-letter day in me career.'

From Foley Street they made good speed along Regent Street and Piccadilly, past the gas-lit restaurants and theatres. Ponsonby strove to arrange his thoughts and eliminate the non-essentials. What he had learned wasn't much, but one item was significant. According to Joe, Hastings had placed his plot in the hands of his agent, a Captain Tim McClune. He was an Irishman, a cool and resolute customer, and all Joe knew about him was that the

McClune family had been virtually wiped out in the Irish famine of twenty years ago. Joe reported that Tim lived at 42 Baker Street. Whether in a house or in rooms, he didn't know.

That was about the sum total, the fruit of an evening's work. Once inside the palace, he went directly to the room he used as his quarters there (he *lived* at Windsor Castle). The clock showed 10 pm. On the baize-covered table that he used for his desk he saw a sealed envelope with the word '*Urgent*' scrawled on it. It was a telegraphic message from Knollys, apparently sent when the Prince's train was a couple of hours out of London, and it differed from other telegraph messages in one respect. It was in Latin; translated, it read:

'Ponsonby – Lady Florence Hastings has warned Chaplin in letter that Hastings has some plan against him involving Prince's train. HRH highly incensed. Skittles Walters is now on train in addition to Hartington and Chaplin. Shall attempt direct telegraphic connection with you this evenng on arrival Kendal.'

Ponsonby smiled rather grimly. The game went on, but was becoming less a game, and his mind kept reverting to McClune. He did not like the sound of him at all.

In the background was the Irish connection. As Her Majesty's equerry and understudy to the Private Secretary, Ponsonby had access to some state papers, although not all by any means, and he had been uneasy ever since he had grasped the ramifications of the Irish story. He had been less than twenty years old at the time of the appalling failure of the Irish potato crop which had cost so many lives and driven so many Irishmen abroad; and even before the famine, they were being driven off their land. That Irishmen were now seeking revenge, not to mention freedom, was not unnatural.

But the bitterness had ascended to a new plateau following the close of the American Civil War and the disbanding of the armies. The Fenian Society, organized in the United States, was swinging into action, and disbanded Irish-American army officers – Fenian agents – had been making their way to Ireland and England. Within the last few months, there had been Fenian plots to seize Chester Castle and to blow up Clerkenwell Prison, and there had been a desperate rescue attempt at Manchester. Threats had been made on the life and person of the Queen – which as usual and as always, she ridiculed. She would take none of it seriously. General Grey, her secretary, on the other hand, took all of it seriously.

He drummed his fingers on the table. The hands of the clock were moving remorselessly forward. The Queen's own telegraph operator, Gooch, was at Balmoral; he travelled with her whenever she was away for a long period. Who had recorded the Knollys message? It had been a good job. He recalled having seen a pimply-faced youth in the telegraph-room at times. He went out to look for a guard.

'Hale's the young fellow's name, sir,' said the guard when he found him. 'Clever with his hands, smart in the upper storey, too, so Mr Gooch tells me. Mr Gooch has taken a fancy to him and has been giving him a bit of training. He's one of the footmen.'

'He is?' exclaimed Ponsonby. In a world of dog eat dog, the evidence of a helping hand shone like a beacon. 'Well, I need Hale just as fast as possible.'

'Very good, sir,' and the guard was as good as his word. Hale came along shortly at the double, buttoning up his coat. Ponsonby wasted no time. 'Hale, you can do me a big favour. Act as operator.' He told him what he wanted.

Hale pulled switches. Clicking started. In a few minutes came the word : 'Kendal is waiting.'

'Good. Here is the first message : "Ponsonby to Knollys. Informant says Hastings's agent, McClune, has taken over plans. May be Fenian. Nature of plans unknown. Precautions definitely advisable in view of happenings at Clerkenwell, Chester, Manchester." '

There was a pause. Clickings resumed. 'Message received. Understood. For your information, Tennyson is here and will accompany Prince. We will obtain pilot engine as precaution. Will be on guard. Knollys.' Now there was no more that he could do until tomorrow, Ponsonby decided. He gave Hale a pat on the shoulder, and left the room.

In far-away Kendal, however, Knollys found himself with a problem. Pilot engines don't grow on trees. The general superintendent of the northern division of the London and North Western Railway was reached with a lot of difficulty and at a late hour in the evening; he was more than eager to accommodate members of the Royal Family. It was considered good business, although no one really made any money out of it, and if the slightest detail went wrong there was the devil to pay. Yet here was a request for a pilot engine to appear at Kendal at 8 a.m. the following morning, a matter of hours hence !

The request came by telegraph from Kendal Castle and the response, sent the same way, consisted of a two-word sentence:

'Regret impossible.'

Knollys naturally wasn't going to take this at its face value, so he retorted :

'Matter of highest importance.' He decided this was about as far as he could go. Of course, if he had used a phrase such as 'Sovereign's safety involved', the reaction would have been overwhelming and instantaneous. But as yet all was conjecture; in addition, the less attention centred on the train the better – as long as Skittles was a passenger on it. The possibilities of the newspapers getting hold of *that* story were chilling.

A delay ensued as the superintendent considered. This was becoming difficult. He made a counter-offer :

'Can supply pilot at a later hour in morning or can have one ready when train reaches Carlisle.'

The superintendent then had a brain-wave. He remembered the Earl of Kendal. Although he and all other railwaymen were opposed to having amateurs dabbling in the running of trains, there was a difference in running an engine *without* a train. The message continued :

'Hesitate to offer this suggestion, which may be entirely out of order, but if Earl of Kendal will volunteer engine and services as far as Carlisle this railway will consent to arrangement without of course in any way assuming liability.'

Knollys whistled. This could be a way out. There was no need even to ask Porky what he thought about it. It was one of his life dreams to be able to get out on the main line, beyond the confines of his own acres, yet he had never been able to do it.

This time Knollys went a step further. He struck a really big blow for Porky. 'Thank you. Your suggestion accepted. If Earl assumes responsibility he will wish to proceed entire way to Ayrshire Castle. Will you make necessary arrangements with Caledonian Railway for this purpose?'

A pause followed. The answer came: 'Yes, LNWR will make necessary arrangements with Caledonian.'

Another pause, and then:

'Experienced stoker will be required for pilot engine.'

Knollys hummed a tune. He knew the answer to this one. The Earl had his own stoker who doubled as a butler (or vice versa). His name was Elliot. It was a sharing of interests between master and servant not encountered hitherto in the history of the peerage. The Duke of Bridgewater had retainers who worked canal boats. But only one retainer stoked a railway engine: Elliot.

When Knollys returned to join the others he found them dancing. Tennyson was the partner of Skittles in what seemed to be a minuet. Skittles was laughing wildly and a glance towards the corner where a table was well provided with bottles, decanters, and glasses, showed the Prince applauding in high glee. The poet was attempting some refined steps, but was rolling like a sailor in a storm.

Porky was doing his best to act as host and was the only serious one in the party. His face lit up when Knollys broke the news.

'Post of honour. All mine,' said Porky proudly.

As dawn came to Kendal Castle, the servants began bringing round the morning tea; the clocks showed 6.45, and the train was to leave at eight o'clock.

The Poet Laureate, enormous in a white nightgown in a gigantic bed, had poetry on his mind despite the ardours of the night before. He peered out of his window and saw the battlements. A line occurred to him:

'The splendour falls on castle walls'

and he thought he would be able to do something with it. Hartington and Skittles, in adjoining rooms, managed to look decorous as well as relaxed. The Prince was weary; he feared the shape of things to come. Frankly, he feared his mother. As he sipped his tea, he decided that, on arrival at Ayrshire Castle, he would keep his own coach and send the rest of the train on to the Highlands immediately – with one exception. Tennyson would remain. Tennyson would impress the Queen and (he hoped) turn her thoughts in the direction of other, higher, and more distant things. This was at variance with his original plan. He had actually thought that he could 'drop off' at Ayrshire, as it were, for about three hours, in the meantime holding the entire train, as well as his friends, on a siding until he was through. While he worshipped at the shrine of Albert, they could play a few rounds of cards and have a few drinks. Alas for such hopes.

There was half an hour left for breakfast when all were assembled downstairs. Two vast sideboards were covered with dishes – bacon, ham, steaks, kidneys, chops, fish, eggs, porridge. They helped themselves. Other details of the departure, baggage-loading and so on, were already under way. So they moved off on time. When they got to the main line the pilot engine chugged ahead, about three-quarters of a mile in front of the Prince's train. The Earl took off his coat and sniffed the air. They were moving through Cumberland towards the border.

'The post of honour!' he declared again.

'The post of honour is the post of danger, my lord,' said Elliot.

'You anticipate trouble?'

'Who can tell, Elliot? Who can tell?'

4

The Queen, travelling southward, was not in the best of moods, and what she found on her arrival at Aberdeen (the first stop) did not improve things.

She was prepared for little courtesies even though they were a waste of time. The general manager of the Deeside Railway would be replaced by a representative of the Caledonian Railway and he, too, would in turn be replaced by an official of the Highland Railway when they arrived at Stanley Junction. A few perfunctory bows handled this.

But to her dismay she found the Aberdeen platform lined with people – entirely uncalled for in her opinion, since this was not an official visit to Aberdeen nor even a visit at all. It was clear they were bent on an address of welcome of some sort. One of them was holding a parchment scroll.

She shuddered. Five years ago she had attended an unveiling of a statue of dear Albert in this city and she had never forgotten the circumstances. To start with, she had been terribly nervous – Albert had been dead only two years. It was raining torrents. The site of the statue was not to her liking although chosen by the sculptor himself. There didn't seem to be anyone in charge to guide her or tell her precisely what to do and where to go. But worse was to come. The principal of the university had droned a prayer interminably (or so it seemed) while the assembly stood uncovered, as the rain lashed their faces. She herself had been so incapable of concealing her irritation that the Press had noticed and commented on it. She remembered in particular the perceptive story in the *Scotsman*.

As the train came to a stop it was John Brown – as usual – who was first out of his compartment and into hers to see if he could be of service, and – as usual – she did not attempt to conceal her feelings from him. She feared the worst, or to put it bluntly, she just feared Aberdeen. There was no need to *say* what she was thinking; her expression was enough.

'Puir woman,' responded John Brown, who understood instantly. 'Well, they'll not be worrying you.' He dropped back on to the platform, and, before either General Grey or Dr Jenner, who were walking up, grasped what was happening, he had taken the scroll out of the hand of the dignitary. 'Her Majesty thanks ye,' he said, 'and she'll be reading it on the train the while.' A few minutes later he handed the document to Her Majesty, who received it without comment.

'Did you see that!' hissed Dr Jenner.

'Keep your thoughts to yourself, my friend,' advised General Grey. 'Be friendly. Be solicitous. Remember the palace favourite is always with us – one of the facts of life.'

'Bah!' said Jenner. 'I'm a doctor, not a courtier.' At that moment he glanced into the compartment of Sergeant-footman Collins. 'Is this man asleep? What's the matter here?' he asked. The sergeant-footman was stretched out at full length, breathing hoarsely. Jenner poked him gently with his cane. 'Collins, wake up, man!'

Collins didn't stir. 'Something wrong,' said Jenner, opening the door. He made a hurried examination; John Brown, who missed nothing, now joined them. Jenner ignored him, and turned to General Grey. 'We've got to get this man out of here immediately. He needs medical attention.'

'Anything that will put that laddie out of commission is serious,' was Brown's comment. 'He's never had an ill moment in ten years ... I'll do his duties for him such as they are, and I'll inform Her Majesty. I can guard her just as well as Collins can, indeed better.'

Porters were quickly summoned; Jenner conferred with the station-master and left directions; the helpless man was lifted out; whistles blew; doors slammed; and the train was on its way again.

The sergeant-footman was not aware of any of this, of course. He was oblivious to earthly affairs. He failed to see the dignitaries who had been on the platform break up into small groups and wend their way to daily occupations. And he entirely missed the fairy appearance of the city – the glistening effect of early morning sunlight on buildings of granite and mica (although without sun, the place looked dismal). He missed also a personal tribute. The Queen might dislike Aberdeen, but Aberdeen liked the Queen, and anyone who was close to her basked in reflected glory. The sergeant-footman became a celebrity, and the procession to the Royal Infirmary on Woolman's Hill was a distinguished one. On arrival, he was placed in a private room. A nurse was assigned to him.

The doctor who received the first summons to the scene was a

Dr Kelso, a young man with a dour face. He was surprised when he saw city councillors and magistrates in the corridor. He listened intently to the station-master's story, closed the door behind him, and began his examination. He became quite puzzled. After a lapse of about ten minutes, during which he gazed out of the window, he walked to the rear of the building and disappeared into the office of Dr Drummond. Dr Drummond's feats of diagnosis had been likened to second sight in some quarters, because of their accuracy, coupled with the fact that Dr Drummond was close to being blind, as well as extremely old. He had been an army surgeon at the Battle of New Orleans in 1814, where he had seen the decimation of his beloved Highlanders.

The old man was at his desk, peering at a piece of paper through a magnifying lens. Both paper and lens were only an inch or two from his bushy eyebrows. He listened without comment to Kelso, then rose and ambled after him.

His method of inspection was well known in the hospital, his large red nose, bushy eyebrows and sensitive hands seemed to be travelling all over the torso of the patient, crabwise as it were, and all at once. After ten more minutes, more tests, and a trip back to his office, the doctor was ready.

'Laudanum or something similar,' he said. 'The man either took it by mistake – which is unlikely – or someone gave it to him. If so, he was drugged.'

'Well I'm damned,' said Kelso. 'The authorities had better hear about this.'

'They had indeed.'

The station-master had returned to his duties. Dr Kelso, therefore, decided to walk to the station, a mere half-mile away, by a route that took him past the statue of Prince Albert. Five years had passed since he had watched the unveiling in a rainstorm. He had been a student then, often without enough to eat. He shut those memories from his mind, and turning into the station found the station-master and passed on his information.

'We will send on a message immediately,' said the station-master. 'To Dr Jenner, I presume?'

'Whatever's proper,' said Dr Kelso. 'This is really out of my field, but, yes – *I* would address myself to Dr Jenner. But if the message is going from *you*, should not the report go to Her Majesty or to General Grey? This involves a person in the Royal Household.'

In the end it was decided to bracket Jenner and Grey and they concocted a simpler message:

'Collins suffering from overdose of laudanum or similar. Condition not critical but should be held under observation. You may wish to investigate.'

'That sounds businesslike, and, as it should be, not *too* alarming,' said the station-master, reading it for the fourth or fifth time. 'This will go to Ayrshire Castle, no doubt. You would not contemplate stopping the train for such as this, would you?'

Dr Kelso shook his head.

He had only one suggestion before wending his way back to the infirmary. 'Just as a precaution it might be well to duplicate the message to London – to Buckingham Palace.'

He knew nothing about the world of royalty but somehow just on account of making the suggestion he felt that for a few fleeting seconds he had been close to power and influence. Some twenty miles down the line Jenner and Grey were still discussing the Collins affair. 'Very puzzling,' mused Jenner. 'I didn't get an opportunity to look at him closely. I wish I had. I must make a point of finding out as soon as possible.'

Grey shook his head. He got the drift of it but he was growing deaf and hated to admit it. He was absorbed in his own thoughts. It was he who had insisted, almost on bended knees, on the enlargement of the guard at Balmoral, Buckingham Palace, Windsor Castle, and Osborne House. Only the Duke of Cambridge had supported him. The Queen had become quite stubborn; and then he had done what few in court circles would have dared to do. He had said: 'Then I take no further responsibility for your safety, ma'am.' The Queen backed down; but things had never been quite the same since. Aloud, he said. 'Jenner, a great wrong has been done to the Irish. One day the chickens will come home to roost.'

Jenner nodded. 'What put you on that chain of speculation? Surely not Collins . . .'

'That has been my chain of speculation, as you put it, for several years.'

The train clanked onward.

Lady Jane Ely sat by herself in a compartment, pondering her fate and her future. Her fate was that she was a widow and her future was tied entirely to the whims of the Queen. She was a lady-in-waiting, or more exactly, a Lady of the Bedchamber, and she was not a clever woman.

In the compartment adjoining, the Queen's two dressers, one old, one young, talked in fits and starts; but they hadn't much in common apart from the work in hand. Travel – for them – was trouble. On the last trip – a long one – the Queen had wished to retire early. There was no station near, so the train was stopped at the top of a high, exposed hill. The wind whistled dreadfully. Snow was falling. They (the dressers) lowered themselves to the ground, and stumbled along the tracks to undress Her Majesty . . . The older dresser, Emile Dittweiler, had been taking care of the Queen for nearly a quarter of a century. She spoke with a thick German accent, and wore thick glasses.

The younger dresser, Mary Nolan, was quite new, indeed an unknown quantity. She was being tried out. Manchester was her native town and the Queen had become entranced with her, so it was said, because she was beautiful. Beauty at any of the royal palaces or castles was rare, except at formal entertainments. The marble halls mostly were filled with dull shapes. Joy was not encouraged. How was it that Mary Nolan seemed to have caught the royal eye? Some said it happened on a day when the Queen was seen to smile at some fleeting memory of Albert. Some subtle chemistry had been present at the time: after all, it is the *nuances* that are important.

At 11.25 a.m. the Queen's train pulled slowly into Stanley Junction, just as the Earl of Kendal on the opposite side of the platform puffed in with his pilot engine, followed shortly by the Prince's train. Everywhere blinds were drawn – on the Queen's coach, and, across the way, on the Prince's coach, Hartington's coach, and Chaplin's coach.

The Prince's train drew to a stop, a door was opened and the Prince stepped out on to the platform. Immediately behind him was Tennyson in a cloak and broad-brimmed black hat that made him look like an oversized operatic figure. The Prince led the way to his mother's coach. John Brown stood at the door; the Prince looked through him. He entered, and, embracing his mother, was at once transformed into the schoolboy in the presence of the teacher. The Queen, for her part, reverted to that role as if she lived it : 'Bertie,' she said, 'you have been smoking !'

Then she caught sight of Tennyson.

'My dear Mr Tennyson ! A most pleasant surprise.' The Poet Laureate bent low and kissed the plump little hand. He had been smoking like a chimney ever since leaving Kendal, but somehow the Queen failed to take note of it. She added, 'What brings you here?'

'My humble tribute to a beloved Prince, Your Majesty.'

The answer pleased her. She was quite moved by his devotion to the memory of the Prince Consort. And nothing could be more natural than that Mr Tennyson should be invited to be *her* guest on the last leg of the trip, from Stanley Junction to Ayrshire Castle, and that the Prince, although not exactly invited in as many words, should politely decline anyway and return to his coach. No great pressure was put on him to do otherwise.

His Royal Highness wiped his brow with a large handkerchief as he recrossed the platform. Midway he encountered the engine-driving Earl who was walking round in his shirtsleeves, wearing a workman's hat. The effect on the Prince was immediate. As far as he was concerned, the correct uniform, the correct clothes, the correct decorations – these were things that *really* mattered. He turned red in the face. 'Porky, what the devil do you mean appearing like that?'

The Earl wasn't in the least perturbed. 'That's all right, sir. Warm work, that's all.' He waved a signal to Elliot, and put on his coat again.

The Prince disappeared into his coach. At another point on the platform the Caledonian Railway official who had replaced the Deeside Railway official now gave way in turn to an official of the Highland Railway. He happened to be a famous character – a rough diamond, as the saying goes, whose silk hat and frock-coat looked as though they had been slept in (or on). His name was Gilkes.

In a minute or two, shunting began, and the two trains were linked together ... And then they were moving, with the Earl again travelling ahead, in the post of honour.

As the scenery slid by, the Queen smiled beatifically on the Poet Laureate. She was not alone. That would be unthinkable. A companion had been summoned, and that meant Lady Ely, sitting in a shadow with a polite half-smile. A splendid figure of a mar, thought the Queen. Nobility in the face. A bluffness that reminded her of dear John Brown. She wondered if she could ask him to recite a verse or two of *The Lady of Shalott*, one of her favourites, and one of Albert's. She asked; she received.

The organ voice rose and fell, sonorous, subtle, emotional, pervasive:

> 'On either side the river lie
> Long fields of barley and of rye,
> That clothe the wold and meet the sky;
> And thro' the field the road runs by
>   To many-tower'd Camelot.
> And up and down the people go,
> Gazing where the lilies blow
> Round an island there below
>   The Island of Shalott.
> Willows whiten, aspens quiver,
> Little breezes dusk and shiver
> Thro' the wave that runs forever
> By the island in the river
>   Flowing down to Camelot.
> Four gray walls and four gray towers,
> Overlook a space of flowers,
> And the silent isle imbowers
>   The Lady of Shalott.'

The louder passages thrilled her; the softer ones caused a tear to run down her cheek. Was not she, the Queen, also alone? Enclosed by grey walls and towers? She leaned forward. 'Thank you, Mr Tennyson.'

'Your obedient servant, ma'am.'

There was a pause. The Queen was curious about the life this man led. How did he happen to be at Stanley Junction – with Bertie of all people, who had no use at all for poets? She began gently. His answers couldn't have been more frank. When he came to the Kendal Castle episodes he was in high humour. He had found the company excellent ... Lord Hartington ... Mr Chaplin ... and a young lady – delightful – who seemed to be known as Skittles ...

'Skittles, Mr Tennyson? How odd.'

'All I heard, ma'am, all I heard, although now and again it was Skitsie.' He smiled reminiscently.

'Oh come, she must be somebody and come from somewhere.'

'Ma'am, I asked her point blank, for that's my way. The only answer I got was "I'm a guest."'

'And she is now on this train?'

'Oh yes – I mean, I suppose so.'

The Queen had a glint in her eye and more questions, many more. The name struck a chord, a harsh and vibrant one. But she was interrupted. The brakes began to grind as the train moved through a marvellous piece of countryside. The hills were closing in. Suddenly they seemed to meet in a deep chasm on each side of the railway. A river struggled for passage among the rocks, now dark and silent, now foaming.

The train was slowing down.

Ponsonby did not wake at the palace as early as he expected on Friday morning. His evening at Mott's had worn him out. He had never felt so tired since those August days thirteen years ago in the Crimean trenches. It was 8 a.m. The Prince's train he knew was to leave Kendal at 8 a.m., and, if he could be sure *that* had been accomplished safely, he would feel a lot better. He dressed quickly and made his way to the telegraph room. Hale was already there.

There were inconclusive clickings for ten minutes, and then the instrument started to make some sense. 'Train left promptly,' Hale deciphered.

'Did they have a pilot engine?' asked Ponsonby.

'Yes, they had a pilot engine. Driver, the Earl of Kendal.' Ponsonby expressed surprise. Hale evidently passed this to the other end of the line which replied: 'Duke of Sutherland also engine-driver. Popular pastime in highest social circles.' There was a pause; then the instrument continued: 'But expensive.' There was one further effort: 'Duke of Buccleuch is a driver.' Clearly the party at the far end was a Scots humorist, or was devoid of humour altogether.

At breakfast later, where he was glad to be alone, Ponsonby buried his head in *The Times* and mapped out his morning. He had a tidy mind and he had marshalled his thoughts. The hour had come – and it would be overdue – to lay the bits and pieces before the 'authorities'. The story had to be shared, however much the Queen might be offended.

By 9 a.m. he was in a hansom cab on his way to the office of the Home Secretary, who was a young barrister named Gathorne-Hardy. He discovered the Home Secretary was out of town.

The time was 9.40 a.m.

The way now pointed to the Prime Minister. Here Ponsonby hesitated. Mr Disraeli had held office for only a few months, and from his ringside seat at the palace Ponsonby had ample opportunity to observe his performances with the Queen. To say that the Prime Minister laid it on with a trowel understated the case. Adulation, devotion, flattery – there seemed to be no limits. All part of the act, of course, and yet, and yet ... He wanted a little more time to think, and on an inspiration told the driver to make a detour to Baker Street. Number 42 was the residence of Captain Tim McClune, and at least he would have the satisfaction of knowing what the place looked like.

It was one of those London days that make one feel good to be alive; he felt his spirits rising as the cab moved down Oxford Street and turned into Baker Street. As they turned the corner, he found himself gazing at the back of a figure that seemed familiar.

The hair was bushy. The man looked sideways to reveal a wild beard and broken spectacles. Incongruously he carried a cane ... It was O'Toole, the former telegraphist whom he had met the previous evening at Mott's.

Ponsonby rapped on the roof and told the driver to slow down. O'Toole was striding briskly. It was clear he knew his way and where he was going. He halted, turned into a doorway, and pulled a bell. The number on the lintel, in brass numerals, was 42. A few seconds elapsed before the door opened and a woman let him in.

'Keep going,' Ponsonby told the driver. A hundred paces or so beyond and out of view of the windows at 42, Ponsonby told him to turn in the street and pull up at the opposite pavement. Now he was facing south, towards the sound of the traffic in Oxford Street. It was an excellent vantage point.

Perhaps fifteen minutes elapsed before O'Toole appeared again. He had an envelope in his hand, which he opened and peered inside. He slipped it into his coat pocket. Without hesitating a moment, he began a resolute march to Oxford Street, his shoulders hunched forward.

'Follow that man,' said Ponsonby.

At the corner, O'Toole crossed Oxford Street.

'Turn left,' said Ponsonby, making a quick bet with himself as to where O'Toole was bound. He leaned back with his head behind the window. 'Slow up' was the next order. O'Toole, it was pretty clear, was waiting for a bus. Fortune was kind. At that instant one of the Thomas Tilling omnibuses arrived and O'Toole jumped aboard. A quick inspection of the sign on the side showed that it would take him close to Foley Street. Ponsonby was sure that O'Toole was bound for Mott's. Somehow he knew it.

The morning was fast disappearing.

At 12.15, Ponsonby put in another appearance in the palace telegraph room and, after only a little wait, got the message that both trains had arrived safely at Stanley Junction.

It was now 12.30 p.m.

He said to Hale, 'I hope to see the Prime Minister. You can reach me if you need to.'

Mr Disraeli was seated by a window of a private dining-room at the Athenaeum attacking some turbot, which was a favourite of his, when he glanced across Pall Mall and saw Ponsonby climbing out of a hansom cab.

'There's Ponsonby,' he told Monty Corry, his private secretary, who was sitting opposite. 'I thought he was at Balmoral.'

'No. Some relative or other died. He had to come to London.'

'Grey is up there I take it?'

'Yes.'

'I doubt if Grey's health will allow him to last long. Ponsonby will soon be succeeding him as Private Secretary. Did you know it was Grey who gave me my first defeat for Parliament? Nearly forty years ago. I opposed him at High Wycombe. I lost by twelve votes to twenty; it was the last election under the old system. Those twelve votes cost £500. Alas, it wasn't enough ... Ah, the speeches I used to make in front of the Red Lion Inn at High Wycombe. I was for the people, of course.' He sipped a glass of claret. 'And now I have climbed to the top of the greasy pole.' He smiled sardonically. 'They have even permitted me to join the Athenaeum!'

A steward advanced on them. 'Colonel Ponsonby wishes to see you, sir. He says it is a matter of importance.'

The Prime Minister raised an eyebrow slightly, which was as near as the mask-like face ever got to a change of expression. 'Bring him in,' he said. The steward departed.

'If Ponsonby says it's important, it is important,' observed Monty. 'He must have come in here from Number 10. By Gad, I must say that is unusual.'

Ponsonby arrived, was offered a seat and accepted; he declined some claret. 'If you don't mind,' he began, 'I'll tell the story in sequence.'

He presented the facts he had gathered, without embellishment, including his discovery of the former palace telegraph operator at Captain McClune's home. He was not an inspired story-teller, but his words had the ring of truth. He held Disraeli and Monty Corry spellbound.

'You were right in bringing this to me,' was Disraeli's first comment. 'I'm uneasy. I don't like it. What is your latest news of the train?'

'Safe at Stanley Junction thirty-five minutes ago.'

'How much of the journey remains?'

'Perhaps one hour and a half.'

'What railway is it?'

'The Highland Railway. Previously the Caledonian. Before that, the Deeside.'

'Time is decidedly against us,' said the Prime Minister, half to himself. 'We must ask ourselves, what do we really know? An idiot member of the nobility is threatening to behave like a bigger idiot than usual. Beyond that, is there some larger, different design? I grant you the Fenian inferences. There is a residue of hate there that will be with us for a century, if not longer. But what has the Marquis of Hastings got to do with Fenians? So far as I know, all the Marquis is interested in is horses and drink.'

The Prime Minister looked thoughtfully out on to Pall Mall, when something in the street caught his attention. 'Good God, I believe we are having a Ducal visitation.'

They all looked out of the window. Below, in all his war paint, was the Duke of Cambridge. He wore a peaked hat with plumes that fluttered in the breeze. Medals, decorations hung all over him. His rotund face was as red as his uniform.

'What the devil brings our royal friend to the Athenaeum of all places?' continued Disraeli. 'He doesn't read books, he doesn't like art and he doesn't converse. Is he coming to see *me*?'

He was. In no time the steward came alongside and whispered: 'The Duke of Cambridge wishes to see you, sir.'

'Bring him in.'

The Duke was a bellicose figure when he entered the room and found the three men standing. The Prime Minister's salutation was a little gem of acting, a touch of reverence proper to a Royal Duke in contrast to an ordinary duke. For a moment it seemed to have little effect.

His Royal Highness was excited. 'Don't tell me I haven't warned you, sir, and warned everyone, including the Queen. We may have treason if not revolution on our hands. This telegraphic message, sir: the lines to Balmoral cut in two places!'

The Prime Minister drew a quick breath but outwardly appeared as inscrutable as ever. 'What telegraphic message?'

'This, sir, this,' retorted the Duke, waving McCullogh's message. 'I received this at the Horse Guards within the half hour. I made an attempt to communicate with Balmoral, but was informed there is no communication. What do you know about the Queen's safety?'

'The Queen isn't at Balmoral,' replied Disraeli. 'Ponsonby, what do you make of it? Allow me to see the message.' The Duke handed it over.

Ponsonby studied it ... 'From Cowell to Grey ... and it says forwarded by McCullogh. I don't understand that. McCullogh is station-master at Ballater ... And if the telegraph lines are down, how did this get through?'

'This puts an entirely different complexion on things,' put in Disraeli.

'What do you mean by that?' rumbled the Duke. 'You've had some prior information?'

The Prime Minister hesitated. A number of thoughts ran through his mind. The Duke was half a century behind the times and he was happiest when regiments, dressed like cockatoos, paraded like robots in useless evolutions. Yet he had the ear of the Queen, not to mention a hierarchy of senior officers who had purchased their commissions – and the investment for a commission was a large one. The most recent price for a colonelcy in a cavalry regiment was £14,000. That was the quotation from the unofficial auction room in Charles Street, in Mayfair, as related to him by Monty, who was his eyes and ears – as well as being a gay dog about town. The Duke's potential for trouble was considerable. What to reveal to him, and when, was a problem. These speculations occupied only a second, but before the Prime Minister could speak, the steward interrupted for a third time. It was as though a bell were tolling.

'What is it *now*?' asked Disraeli.

It was a message for Ponsonby. 'A young man to see you, sir. From the palace.'

'Where is he?'

'Downstairs, sir.'

'I'll see him there.'

Ponsonby followed the steward down the corridor past an engraving of Sir Walter Scott, one of the early members. He had often wondered what Scott would have thought about Disraeli being blackballed for nearly thirty years. In an ante-room by the entrance-hall was Hale, and he knew instantly from his expression that something was seriously wrong.

'What's the matter, Hale?'

'I have a message and a report, sir,' and he handed over the communication devised by Dr Kelso in Aberdeen, reporting that the Queen's sergeant-footman Collins was a victim of laudanum.

Ponsonby, who had travelled many hundreds of miles with Collins and knew him to be as strong as a horse, grasped the implication immediately. But the big shock was yet to come.

'The train seems to be held up somewhere, sir,' said Hale.

'Held up! What do you mean?'

'Well, it didn't arrive where it should have.'

'Be specific.'

'Very good, sir. The station at Blair Atholl was supposed to report when the train passed through. It didn't pass through. It didn't get there.'

'Is Blair Atholl the next station beyond Stanley Junction?'

'No, sir. There's several.'

'Where was the last report from? Where was the train last seen?'

'Station called Pitlochry, sir.'

The train had stopped or been stopped then. Something was going on. Ponsonby dared not imagine what.

He ran out of the room, but slowed to a walk when he realized it would be folly to alarm club members, and, through them, the public. It needed great discipline to walk. He wished he could pull the Prime Minister out of the room and talk to him privately. It wasn't feasible. He broke the news to the three of them. The first repercussion came from the Duke, whose cheeks had been puffing and blowing throughout the recital.

'Treason it is,' he bellowed. 'Treason!' He lapsed into a flow of German, of which only part was translatable. The Prime Minister gave the impression of being coiled up'like a spring. He walked across the room and pulled a bell-cord. Once again the steward appeared.

'A guide to Scotland as quickly as possible. Fast!' he ordered.

Since the club library was in an adjoining room only a few seconds elapsed before the guide-book was in his hands.

He riffled through the pages. 'Here! ... Stations on the Highland Line ...' He began enunciating the names precisely; they almost took on the character of biblical places: 'Murthly; Dunkeld; Dalguise; Guay; Ballinluig; Pitlochry; Killiecrankie; Blair Atholl ...'

He continued: 'The train has been reported at Pitlochry, but not at Blair Atholl. Obviously it must be near or at Killiecrankie ...'

He flipped some more pages ... 'I read from page 334.' He looked at the back of the book. '*Blake's Guide to Scotland*. About two miles beyond Pitlochry, the railway proceeds through the historically famous pass of Killiecrankie by a magnificent viaduct of ten arches, fifty-four feet high and thirty-six feet span, and, by keeping upon the left-hand side of the railway carriage one may see as much of the grandeur of this remarkable piece of Highland scenery as will satisfy those who are neither able nor willing to visit it on foot ...'

He shut the book.

'There are only three or four miles between most of the stations on the Highland Line ... It cannot be long before we have news ... Gentlemen, will you accompany me to Downing Street. Your Royal Highness, if we could use your equipage? Colonel Ponsonby, your services are at our disposal, I'm sure ...'

They marched through the entrance-hall, where Ponsonby had a word with the waiting Hale. 'Report to 10 Downing Street,' he told him. The Duke's carriage was superb. Large coats of arms, hand painted, embellished both doors. Two guardsmen were on the box, two in the rear. Two guardsmen on horseback acted as escort. The Duke's equerry contributed to the scenic splendour ...

At Number 10, the Prime Minister led the way past a hall-porter in a hooded chair, through a green baize door, down a corridor into an ante-room, where there were a grandfather clock and a bust of Wellington, and then into his study, which was where the cabinet sometimes held its meetings. He warmed his hands briefly at the fireplace and sat down at his desk.

'Only essentials are important,' he said. 'Immediate question: the safety of the Sovereign. If she *is* safe, we have a breathing space. If not . . .' He left the speculation hanging in the air.

'Our immediate need: telegraphic communication.' He paused for a second. Ponsonby interrupted, 'I had the palace operator report here in case he could be useful.' He did not feel it necessary to add that the operator was a footman and an amateur.

Disraeli nodded. 'Good. Our telegraph office is next door, at Number 11. Monty, show him the way. He's outside, I assume . . . I wish continuous reports from the Highland Railway. Any and all reports . . .' He looked at the clock in the corner. The time was 2.55 on a warm autumn afternoon. Outside the window was a view of the terrace and the trees in the garden.

Monty departed and the Prime Minister pulled a bellcord. A young man responded, either a clerk or a private secretary.

The Prime Minister collected his thoughts. 'I want a special train assembled instantly at Euston station. For possible departure within the hour. You will accept no excuses.' He scribbled some words on a small sheet of paper with the large letters that were his trade-mark. 'This will suffice. Use it as you see fit. What sort of train is immaterial. What I would *prefer*' – he stroked his cheek – 'a director's coach, one regular coach, two private coaches . . . They will ask the destination, naturally. For the moment, tell them Scotland. Nothing further . . .'

He looked round the room.

'Your Royal Highness. Your counsel, sir?'

The Duke snorted. 'Surround the area with troops, thousands of 'em. If the scoundrels have as much as moved an inch in the direction of Her Majesty, mow 'em down.'

'And how long would it take, sir, to assemble these troops in the Killiecrankie area?'

'A day. As soon as they could be dispatched from Edinburgh.'

The Prime Minister was paying the Duke the courtesy of listening with profound absorption – or so it appeared – and he nodded his head as though he was listening to the fount of wisdom. What he was thinking was something quite different, and, while the Duke had no inkling of this, it was at once sensed by Monty who was now at the rear of the room, having hurriedly returned from his brief visit to the telegraph office. Disraeli distrusted the Duke's advice on general principles. The prospect of the Duke, as Field Marshal and Commander-in-Chief (and a Royal Duke to boot), on the loose, without restraint, attempting to direct the rescue of the Queen (should any rescue be called for), appalled him. It would be bungled.

'And would your Royal Highness order out the troops now? Would you telegraph a precautionary order? Or do you advise waiting until we have some positive word from the train?'

'Now, dammit, now!' shouted the Duke. 'No precautions. No waiting.'

The Prime Minister addressed Monty. 'Kindly draft a message to the commander-in-chief of the forces in Scotland embodying the Duke's recommendations. Bring it here to him. Quickly.'

Monty left the room. Suddenly the Prime Minister seemed to be struck by a thought. He snapped his fingers, apologized, and left his chair with surprising suppleness. Once outside, he came up with Monty, and, as far as anyone observing the scene would have noticed, he did no more than nod his head, then shake his head. To Monty this conveyed all that was needed. The interpretation: the telegram would give every appearance of going, but it never would; or if it did, it would never arrive; or if it did arrive it would be late or indecipherable. Such was the understanding between Disraeli and his Private Secretary that words were unnecessary.

It would be folly to mount a military campaign to rescue the Queen without first knowing exactly what was her situation. They saw eye to eye on this, as indeed they did on everything.

5

As the Queen's train neared the little station of Ballinluig, which was a junction of sorts – a tiny branch line reached out tentatively as far as Aberfoyle – two of her staff, General Grey, Private Secretary, and Dr Jenner, physician, drowsed in their compartment. It was elegantly fitted. The doors were padded on the inside and there were arm-rests and head-cushions, and iron and brass lanterns for use in the evening. Had they known it, which they probably didn't – and they couldn't have cared less – the coach had six wheels, five doors on either side, and five ventilators, and it weighed 9 tons 16 cwt.

As the train slowed down and the brakes began grinding, General Grey looked out of the window. He could see the platform round a bend. The station-master was there holding a red flag. A gentleman wearing a tall hat stood beside him.

'They are stopping us!' exclaimed Grey, with surprise.

'Well, why not?' murmured Jenner.

'My dear Jenner, you don't just stop a royal train.'

'Obviously a good reason,' continued Jenner.

'Damned good one, I hope,' said Grey. 'You ought to know *that*, my friend, after what happened at Carlisle last year. You were there and I wasn't.'

Jenner stirred uneasily. 'Oh that! Quite awkward, yes.' The Queen on a trip from Windsor to Balmoral had been told that her coach would not be able to pass under some tunnel or arch on the Caledonian line beyond Carlisle. She had been compelled to get out of her coach in the early hours of the morning and clamber into an unfamiliar one. She was annoyed and protesting. Later – and this was the bad part – she had discovered the exchange was wholly unnecessary. She had never forgotten it, nor had she let anyone else forget it since.

The train came to a stop.

Grey got out. The general manager of the Highland Railway, Mr Gilkes, got out. Brown got out.

The station-master advanced, after first saluting Gilkes.

'General Grey, is it?'

'Yes.'

'This gentleman has an urgent message for you, sir.'

'Indeed. From whom?'

'From the Prime Minister,' said the visitor, an excessively tall man with gaunt cheekbones and a wide Celtic mouth. 'Sent by telegraph to Perth where I received instructions to deliver it to you *personally* as soon as possible.'

'And who are you, sir, if I may ask?'

'I am in the office of the Home Secretary and was temporarily on duty in Perth.' It sounded plausible, and the General was beginning to be conscious of royal eyes gazing at him disapprovingly through the window, which meant that any second John Brown would receive a message, psychic or otherwise, and would begin barking orders.

The visitor handed over a small package and added, 'There are some additional points I have been instructed to bring to your attention, sir – verbally.'

'Then jump in, jump in,' said Grey. 'You are free to travel for a couple of stations, I hope.' He didn't wait for an answer. The door slammed behind them. The train began to move.

The stranger sat down in the middle of the seat opposite to Jenner and Grey, both of whom were by a window.

'Anthony Todhunter is the name, sir,' he began. 'The illustrious Dr Jenner, I presume. I have heard of you. I have seen you in London – from a distance, of course. I had heard you were on this train, occupying this compartment.'

'You did?' commented Jenner. 'How?'

'We have our sources, Doctor . . .' General Grey had just completed disentangling what seemed to be several sheets of parchment from a heavy covering embellished with seals and ribbons of various sorts, when Todhunter exclaimed:

'The verbal part first, if you please.'

The General looked up, surprised, if not a little annoyed. Something about the tone was wrong. A note of warning was in the air, indefinable. But it was too late. Faster than the eye could follow, Todhunter pulled out a couple of pistols from somewhere in his suit, and, almost as quickly, flipped down the two middle arm-rests for ready-made pistol rests.

Grey and Jenner made no movement; they just watched. The scenery sped past at some twenty miles an hour, and they passed through the station of Pitlochry. They had a single thought: they were in the presence of a madman.

Grey was the first to speak. The words were grave, almost kindly:

'You realize this is the royal train? The implications?'

'My dear sir, I'm fully aware of the implication,' exclaimed Todhunter in a sort of ecstasy, twisting and turning, yet at the same time keeping both postols aimed from the convenient level of the arm-rests. 'I know all about the implications or I wouldn't be here. I wouldn't worry, General, about the contents of that missive. Meaningless. The Prime Minister never saw it. He'd be appalled if he did. Not his style at all.'

'What are you after?' asked Jenner.

'Brief question. Fair question,' chortled Todhunter, in the same vein of exuberance. 'All will be made clear. First you will take me to the Prince. That will be the beginning.'

'Damn you and your insolence,' exclaimed Grey. 'That's impossible, unless you are tired of living. There are police officers on this train and some twenty people. Many have handled guns.' He edged forward on his seat and with a side glance at Jenner was preparing to spring.

'Don't.'

Both men halted.

'One shot fired by me will be a signal. *The* signal, if you know what I mean ... Spare the Queen!'

'Spare the Queen,' repeated Grey. 'What are you talking about? A child wouldn't be taken in by that ruse.' Intense emotion seemed to have improved his hearing.

'No ruse,' said Todhunter. He looked out of the window. 'We are approaching the Killiecrankie Viaduct. We are about to stop there. We will visit the compartment of Sergeant-footman Collins. You will see for yourselves.'

'Sergeant-footman Collins isn't on this train,' interjected Jenner.
'I know that. I helped to arrange it,' replied Todhunter.
The train stopped.

A shepherd or a hunter or a fisherman or a crofter viewing it from afar from a distant hill would have seen a toy train – an engine and eight coaches – on a toy bridge. It would have been hard to realize at that distance that the viaduct was fifty-four feet above ground – or that real people were involved in what was going on.

'I said we would stop and we stopped,' said Todhunter gleefully. 'Everything is working. Open that door, Doctor. Step down and await General Grey. Thank you. I have selected *this* side because everyone else will pick the other side. But it makes no real difference.'

A slight wind was blowing along the pass as they got down. The hills were covered with oak, alder and birch, and just below, a dizzy view, was the River Garry. Somewhere up in front and on the other side of the train, they could hear voices. As a military man, General Grey felt a chill down his spine. If the aim was to isolate the train, few better spots existed.

They reached the rear end of the Queen's coach. Todhunter blew once softly on a small whistle. A man's head peered out.

'Grey and Jenner,' said Todhunter, an introduction that in itself implied a great deal: they had been discussed by name and plans laid. The casualness was ominous.

'Let Grey come up,' was the reply.

'It's entirely up to you, General,' put in Todhunter. 'I'm not going to give you orders. You have heard. Now see for yourself.'

The General wobbled a little. There was no step to climb on. He looked around. Todhunter still had the pistols. The man above stretched down a hand. Jenner from below gave him a shove.

What he first saw was not at all what he expected. Boxes were neatly stacked on and under the seat and many on the floor.

'Gunpowder,' said the man. 'More than a quarter of a ton.'

'My God,' said Grey, looking instinctively at the thin partition that separated the Queen's quarters. There was no reassurance there.

'. . . And three sets of fuses,' added the man. 'Electrical fuse. Flint-cap fuse. My own fuse – a pistol with a special bullet.'

'We now go to the Prince,' said Todhunter from below. 'Don't try and be heroic. It won't pay. Do not let Her Majesty leave her coach. We haven't gone to this trouble to let her slip through our hands *that* way. Do not delay . . . I believe she will be safe in your hands . . . Why not ! . . . She is in *our* hands.'

Grey shuddered and let himself to the ground. As he remembered later, what sounded most clearly at that moment was the noise of the river. The river had seen great battles in its time and had run red with blood. Jenner joined him, and they made their way together up front. He whispered to him while Todhunter followed them, his hands clasped behind his back, under his coat-tails. He had concealed his pistols again.

As they circled the engine, they saw the driver at his post.

And who should be there also, further along the line, but Elliot, the butler, dressed according to his own idea of what a stoker should wear, and clutching a red rag in his hand. He had evidently been waving it; and the alarm had stopped the royal train. Just ahead of Elliot was the pilot engine, with the Earl on the footplate. The pilot engine had barely begun to enter the tunnel that separates one end of the Killiecrankie Viaduct from Killiecrankie station when for some reason it had come to a dead stop.

At that moment general manager Gilkes arrived on the scene, angry and bristling. He had a large moustache and a bull neck. 'What's the delay here? What's going on?' He had a few seconds to study Elliot, who looked like no stoker he had seen before. 'Who are you?'

'I stoke for His Lordship, sir.'

'Ha . . .' But fortunately Gilkes recalled in time. There *was* a Lordship in a pilot engine – unbelievable yet true.

'What the devil's the matter?' rasped Gilkes.

'Can't make any headway on the lines, sir. His lordship noticed it about three-quarters of the way across the viaduct. When we got to the tunnel, we stopped. The wheels just spun. Observe the lines for yourself, sir.'

'I can see 'em,' growled Gilkes. 'What's the matter with 'em?' He bent down, muttering, touched the metal, and arose, staring at a finger. It was covered with grease.

'No doubt some sort of practical joke, sir,' was Elliot's next contribution.

'Joke? The devil it is.' Gilkes was becoming apoplectic. 'Get rags. Get this line cleaned. Get sand, get water, get brushes, go up to the station and get help ... You, you.' He pointed at the stoker of the Queen's train and at Elliot. 'This is a black mark against the Highland Railway. It will be years before the Highland recovers from this deed.'

Grey and Jenner had completed their return to the Queen's coach, when Grey saw to his horror that Brown had brought out a folding footstool, which meant that the Queen was about to step down and see for herself what was going on. No doubt she and Tennyson had been discussing the beauties of the scenery. In any case the poet was transfixed; he would follow blindly.

> Revered, beloved – O you that hold
> A nobler office upon earth
> Than arms, or power of brain, or birth
> Could give the warrior kings of old

so he had written in his *Lines to the Queen*. These were his feelings.

'No! No!' shouted Grey to Brown.

'What is it that is troubling you, General?'

'She must not come down!'

'Well, that is exactly what she proposes to do.'

The Queen was standing at the open door, a diminutive figure. Behind her stood the poet. Grey gestured with waving arms. The Queen looked puzzled, as well she might be, but the bull-headed Brown propped up the stool and took a waiting position beside it.

Grey shouted again. 'Take it away!' and, moving into action, he kicked it over and shoved it to one side.

'Ye damn' old fool!' was Brown's response, after he had recovered from his amazement. The two of them began scuffling. Jenner, who, if anything, was as powerful as Brown, struggled to separate them; and from the other direction came the Prince of Wales, puffing and blowing. He had grown increasingly fretful on account of the stop. What he saw made him doubt the evidence of his senses. He turned to Knollys who hurried up behind him: 'That swine Brown is fighting with Grey. The old man's nearly twice his age.'

Knolly plunged in to assist Jenner. He was glad of the chance. The Queen meanwhile had become transformed with fury. Brown had been following her orders – as he always did. He could do no wrong. He was irreplaceable. As for the General, words failed her: with her own eyes she had seen him kick away her footstool.

She called out in her bell-like voice – and it was heard above the din. 'How dare you! Let John Brown alone!' The seething group, which had grown bigger with the addition of a guard and two police officers (Hartington and Chaplin prudently kept out of sight), shuffled into some sort of order. The voice continued: 'Mr Knollys, what business is this of yours? My son, I suppose, put you up to it ... Mr Tennyson, I am mortified. That *you* should see this ...' Her lips were drawn in a tight line. She turned and disappeared into the royal coach.

Tennyson was left at the open door, several feet above the crowd on the viaduct, the centre of all eyes. He was undecided what to do. He typified the tragic muse – tall and sombre, with his black, drooping hat and flowing hair. The lines under his eyes seemed heavy, which could come either from drinking port (his favourite drink) or from looking inwardly at the stars. He felt it unlikely the Queen would now care to resume a conversation on King Arthur and the Knights of the Round Table. Even if she did, the sense of mystery would have vanished, the magic dissolved.

General Grey stared upwards at the poet. Ignoring Brown's grim looks, he grabbed the footstool and used it himself. He climbed the steps and beckoned to Tennyson. The poet bent down.

'The Queen is in awful danger!'

The poet recoiled.

'I must have your ear – instantly. She cannot, she must

not leave this coach. See that she doesn't. Hold your ground!'

He turned to the Prince. 'Sir, I must see you privately immediately.'

'Must?' queried the Prince, who never liked to hear that word addressed to him. He peered peevishly at the General and saw that he was shaking. 'Are you all right? Are you ill?'

'I am not well, sir.'

'What is this all about?'

'It had best wait until we are inside your coach, sir.' At this point the Prince became aware of Todhunter, the incongruous shadow. 'Who is this individual?'

'He is the reason for my urgent request, sir.'

'Most unusual.' The Prince peered at Grey again and evidently became convinced that whatever was afoot was serious. He began the return to his own coach. In the meantime, a couple of men had emerged from the tunnel, coming from Killiecrankie station, armed with rags and buckets of sand. Mr Gilkes continued bellowing orders . . .

Once in his own quarters, the Prince produced a gold watch and examined it pointedly. As he replaced it in his pocket, he was astounded to see the General suddenly leap on the back of the man he had brought along with him and wrap his arms and legs around him. He heard the words: 'He's armed!'

Todhunter's reaction was to attempt to brush off Grey by whirling him around, as well as up and down. An ornate lamp fell with a crash. The Prince's valet came running from the rear of the coach.

A few seconds elapsed while he sized up the scene, then he threw his arms round Todhunter's face, half choking him. Todhunter gave up the struggle and lay draped over a couch. Grey got unsteadily to his feet, and quickly lifted out the two pistols. 'Don't hurt him,' he wheezed to the valet.

'This man was going to shoot me!' exclaimed the Prince. 'Why the devil did you bring him in here?'

'No, sir. Doubt very much he was going to shoot you . . . Yet I daren't take a chance . . . Hope he won't hold this against us . . .'

'You hope *what*?' demanded the Prince, not believing the

evidence of his ears. The exchange was interrupted by the arrival of Knollys, who was fresh from the job of breaking up the other struggle. He was now the bearer of a tale which he found baffling and, indeed, was so full of it that he did not immediately grasp what had been and was now taking place in the Prince's saloon. 'The Poet Laureate,' he declared, 'is standing in front of the Queen's door and won't let anyone in, and, what's more, won't let her out.'

'Let the Poet Laureate stay there! Those are my orders,' said Grey.

The Prince looked more incredulous than before. He opened a drawer in a small side-table, brought out a bottle of brandy, and poured himself a drink. 'Everyone is going mad,' was his comment.

'The madman is here,' responded Grey, pointing at Todhunter. 'This madman and another madman have the Queen a prisoner. This madman has blackmailed me into bringing him here. He's safe, and he knows it. We daren't touch him. His confederate has installed himself in Collins's compartment and is sitting there with a quarter of a ton of gunpowder only a few feet from the Queen.'

The Prince jerked his glass so that half of the drink fell on the floor. He picked up one of the pistols.

'Don't, sir!' cried Grey, alarmed.

'I echo that, sir,' said Todhunter, recovering some of his former manner. 'Her Majesty is a hostage, yes. That is the only reason I dare expose myself here – and General Grey came very, very close to causing a tragic incident. The Queen will not be harmed – provided our orders in future are followed on time, and to the letter.'

'Your *orders*!' repeated the Prince.

'Our orders.'

'What orders?' demanded Knollys.

Todhunter held up his hand, but he still did not seem to be able to control his curiously serpentine movements.

'The instructions are simple. I give you them: Absolute obedience. Do not touch nor hinder me. Do not attempt to rescue her. The Queen will not move from her coach ... Those are general instructions ... Here are some specific instructions: This train is to be backed down the line to Ballinluig. It is to be turned round there and the Prince's section detached. The Queen's section will proceed with all speed to Liverpool. The route will be by Carlisle, Lancaster, Preston ... There will be further instructions later. A gong will act as a warning signal. One stroke: a message. Two strokes: a warning. Three strokes ... I trust you will never hear three strokes.'

The Prince followed him grimly. 'I'll preside at your execution,' was all he could summon up.

Todhunter ignored it. He said, 'You have ten minutes to translate these instructions into action. You or Her Majesty will give the necessary instructions. I have no doubt you will wish to keep this matter to as restricted a circle as possible.'

He reached out and cautiously picked up the pistols. No one stopped him. He put them in his pocket and marched out of the coach.

The Prince was shaking with rage and frustration. He gave the impression that he might be suffering from a stroke. It was Knollys who was the first to recover himself.

'What will *she* do?'

The Prince's frustration increased, if that were possible. 'She'll not listen. She'll not listen ... Will she listen to *you*, Grey?'

The General was well aware that when matters of high importance were concerned the Queen was not only indifferent to her son's counsel, but looked on it as an invitation to do the opposite. On the other hand, he himself was almost in the same predicament. He replied: 'Unfortunately I have just incurred her serious displeasure, sir. As you know, she *will* listen to John Brown. And always to Mr Tennyson.'

'Ah, Tennyson! It may be fate he's with us.' The Prince was pursuing a chain of thought of his own. He jerked himself from his seat, moved quickly outside, and made his way to the Queen's coach. Grey and Knollys followed.

There was the poet and there was John Brown, the two of them deep in conversation. The poet had a genuine liking for the Highlander, which was returned. There was a bond of sympathy between them. John Brown was revealing his anxieties by opening and closing his hands as though he had, or wished he had, someone by the throat. He did not need the Highlander's gift of 'second sight' (if it can be called a gift) to sense that something dark was in the offing. Incidents, seemingly unrelated, were beginning to add up: the tampering with the rails; the appearance of the stranger in the tall hat at the last station; the extraordinary conduct of General Grey; the conference in the Prince's coach ... As soon as he saw the Prince advancing, he greeted him almost with eagerness, a gesture wholly out of character, since for years he had been as contemptuous of His Royal Highness as HRH had been of him.

The Prince for his part was just getting ready to ascend the footstool and either send Brown away or draw Tennyson aside, when he realized the futility of trying to keep Brown out of the picture. Not only would the Queen tell him everything, but she might well call on him for advice. And another thing: Brown was hot-headed, especially when drunk, which was frequently; he might decide on an heroic rescue attempt.

So the Prince addressed the two of them. He spoke earnestly. The poet's face, which was always expressive, began to mirror violent feelings. First, disbelief; this gave way to horror as he looked sideways at the sergeant-footman's compartment. Then devotion as his glance turned in the direction of Her Majesty.

The Prince now knocked on the royal door, entered, and shortly beckoned to Tennyson and Brown.

The Queen was still sitting like a statue, with hands folded in her lap. A formidable statue.

'Well?'

'You are in grave danger, Mother,' began the Prince.

'Indeed?'

Tennyson chimed in with rolling tones: 'The Poet Laureate presents his humble duty, ma'am ...'

The Queen broke in: 'You sound like Mr Gladstone. I prefer Mr Tennyson. What is it?'

A tear rolled down the poet's cheek. 'You *are* in the gravest danger, ma'am.'

'Is this true, Brown? Forgive me, dear Mr Tennyson. He is my protection these days.'

A tear also trickled down the cheek of John Brown. 'Ah, I have let you down, ma'am. There is a damn' villain sitting on the other side of that partition threatening to blow you to Kingdom Come, if you don't do what he says. And he has the gunpowder to do it. We'll circumvent him in the end, never fear, but in the meantime it would be the better part of valour to play for time.'

The Queen gazed uncomprehendingly at the partition.

'The truth, alas, ma'am,' added Tennyson.

'How is this possible?' asked the Queen. 'Where are the police? My attendants: where is Sergeant Collins? Bertie, what have you to say?'

The Prince's mouth opened. Nothing came forth.

'I don't know what they did to Collins,' declared Brown, 'but Dr Jenner had him taken off at Aberdeen. I should have smelled a rat at the time . . .'

'They? Who is they?' enquired the Queen.

Tennyson shook his head. 'We do not know yet.'

The Queen rose to her full height of less than five feet. The musical voice assumed a flinty quality. 'An intruder in my coach! Arrest him! Bring General Grey here.' She turned to Lady Ely. 'Janie, you heard nothing at all about this?'

'Oh no, ma'am.' It was clear that Lady Ely was on the verge of fainting and would be of little use henceforward. The Queen observed her calmly. 'I shall use *your* coach, Bertie,' she said. 'When that villain is removed, I will return.'

The three bearded men facing her – the Prince, Tennyson, and Brown – shook their heads sadly in unison.

'You cannot leave, ma'am,' said Tennyson.

'*I cannot leave*,' repeated the Queen incredulously, emphasizing each word. '*I* cannot leave?'

'Unfortunately, if you do, ma'am, it will be fatal.'

'Who says it will be fatal?' demanded the Queen sharply. 'I have heard these threats before. General Grey and the Duke of Cambridge kept telling me that the Fenians were on their way from Canada to kidnap me at Osborne. I am still waiting for them.'

'Your wait may be over, ma'am,' said Tennyson, ominously, on the inspiration of the moment. The remark clearly shook the Queen.

She sat down and began to sob quietly ... 'Albert would never have let this happen ... Is there nobody ... ?'

'Yes, dearest lady, there is somebody. Somebody will protect you,' roared Tennyson, anticipating the rest of the question. John Brown brought out his flask and poured some whisky into a glass which he handed to the Queen. She sipped it tearfully.

'Tell me all. Tell me the worst,' she said.

When it was over and they had had their say and had a few words together in an undertone, the Prince and John Brown emerged together. Some subtle changes had taken place. The Prince gave the appearance of having assumed command. Throughout his twenty-six years he had been treated as a wayward child. Now, with his mother immobilized, he had become someone who counted, and, in his own mind at least, sovereign *de facto*.

John Brown on the other hand appeared to be in a strange mood as though some fire was burning within. He was muttering to himself. There was a likeness indeed to that other John Brown who was famous (or infamous) on the other side of the Atlantic, who was no relation at all, but who had also a fanatical gleam in his eye as he led the revolt at Harper's Ferry:

> John Brown's body lies a-mouldering in the grave
> But his soul goes marching on.

It had been a terrible wrench for John Brown to leave the Queen's side. Had he just spoken up and said 'I shall stay', the Queen would have nodded agreement as a matter of course. But he knew the meaning of dedication and he saw that if he were incarcerated with *her* he would never be able to strike a blow on *her* behalf. So it was the Poet Laureate who remained behind as confidant and spiritual counsellor, and who could be a better companion in the hour of trial?

'Where the devil is Gilkes?' growled the Prince, as soon as he set foot on the ground. 'Ah there! Gilkes!' The railway official, who was huddled with Dr Jenner, stepped forward.

'How much do you know, Gilkes? I don't want to repeat. I don't want to go into details. Every second counts.'

'Bad mischief ... terrible catastrophe ...' and Gilkes pointed to the kidnappers' compartment.

'Yes, yes ... Gilkes, we are forced to move this train to Liverpool without delay. Now !'

'Liverpool !' repeated the astounded Gilkes. 'That cannot be, surely ! The Highland Railway doesn't run to Liverpool.'

This reaction, which was the automatic one of a practical, provincial railway man, enraged the Prince who was always emotional, but now trebly so. He quivered.

'Damn you,' he bellowed, and, seizing Gilkes by the lapels, he shook him. 'Get the Queen's train to Liverpool. I don't care how you do it ... Back it down the line to Ballinluig ... Unhook my part of it there. No questions. These are orders.'

Gilkes quivered in turn. 'But, sir, all I meant to say, I meant to say ...' Then he realized the hopelessness of it all. He couldn't convey his predicament, and it wouldn't matter if he could. His two men on the engine had never been outside the Highland system. They knew nothing about the vagaries of the route to Liverpool, which was the province of the London and North Western Railway, and there was rugged country in between. The engine should be changed; they would have to take on water; they would need coal.

And there was another problem, familiar to those who handled the details of the Queen's travel, but not to others. It could be spelled out in a couple of words : lavatory arrangements. Stops were planned along the way at discreet intervals, and such stops were usually combined with the serving of lunch or tea or some railway need such as changing an engine. There were certain stations (Perth was an example), which had a royal suite or royal retiring-room, but that was a major junction and a meeting-point of several railways.

The Queen was not absolutely dependent on these stops since there was a lavatory of sorts at one end of her coach, in her dressing-room. However, the tank had to be emptied and the water-closet replenished during the journey, another detail which had to be included in any advance plan, in co-operation with the royal staff.

But now there was no advance plan. No staff work. Not as much as a sandwich was ready for her along the way. The train was being launched into darkness ... All of this flashed through his mind in an instant, and all he could think of to say, inadvisedly, was : 'There is danger to the Queen, sir.' And that did no good at all.

'Danger, you fool,' exploded the Prince. 'Are you telling *me* there is danger?' But he got no further because a booming noise reverberated behind him, making him turn. The skeleton-like face of Todhunter was leaning out of his window – an ugly sight. He held a brass gong and a gong-stick. He had struck once; now he was about to strike a second time. The alarm was strident, alien, effective.

The Prince froze.

Everyone froze.

'Move !' yelled Todhunter.

The door of the Queen's coach flew open. Two figures were heaving and struggling inside – Tennyson and John Brown. The encounter ended with the poet heaving the Scotsman on to the right of way, where his fall was partly broken by the shoulders and arms of the Prince, Jenner and Gilkes who were gathered below, incredulous.

The Poet was breathing heavily. 'He tried to smuggle out the Queen on the other side,' he said, more in sorrow than in anger.

John Brown had wasted no time. He had scuttled under the wheels of the coach to the other side to attempt a direct *coup*. The Queen had been tempted, no doubt. A door quickly opened, and there was the Highlander beckoning, and always to be relied upon. Others failed her; Brown, never. It had been Tennyson who had intervened. And he had saved her life. But whether she knew this, or would believe it, was another matter.

Brown climbed slowly to his feet.

Todhunter rasped : 'Start the train moving.'

Gilkes gave a hopeless gesture and started trotting towards the engine.

What his engine-driver, McCloskey, knew or guessed, he could not imagine. Most of his attention, he was sure, had been riveted on the greased rails in front of him and the cleaning job in progress there. But he must have seen fights and scuffles involving members of the Queen's own party. Gilkes found him a baffled man. He was the oldest driver with the company and he was proud of his selection for the royal train. His moleskin trousers were impeccable. But the occasion had turned into a nightmare. He said: 'Perhaps you'll be so good as to tell me what's happening, Mr Gilkes. I've seen things with my own eyes I never would have believed possible.'

'Never mind that, McCloskey. I'll tell you all in good time. This train is to be backed up to Ballinluig. Now! Get going and stop it this side of the Ballinluig station.'

'Ballinluig! That's where we've just come from,' was the response.

Gilkes looked down the line. The Prince and others were disappearing into his coach. 'Blow your whistle, McCloskey. Move.'

McCloskey began moving. Gilkes waited until he was a hundred yards away, then he clambered aboard the Kendal engine and beckoned the butler-fireman to join him. He motioned the Earl to have his engine follow in the wake of McCloskey. He told the two men what he knew. They received the news in silence. The Earl was impassive by inheritance, the butler by training.

'Your services may be called upon, my lord,' Gilkes concluded.

Kendal nodded gavely. He had a feeling this might be foreordained. He was ready.

The Prince was holding a council of war in his coach. Close to a dozen people were jammed into it, some sitting, some standing – the two policemen, the train guard, Chaplin, Hartington, General Grey, Knollys. Also John Brown. Also Skittles. Everyone looked haggard.

'Liverpool! Why Liverpool?' demanded the Prince.

'The Irish are there,' said Hartington.

The Prince grunted. It was true that hundreds of thousands of starving Irish, driven from their country, had come to England through the port of Liverpool, and while many, if not most, had gone eventually to America, thousands had stayed. The Scotland Road area of Liverpool was peopled with Irish, huddled in shacks and cellars.

'Who knows Liverpool?' the Prince asked.

Skittles raised her hand.

'You?'

'I was born there.' She might have added, but didn't, that she got her name from there. She had worked in a skittle-alley in a Liverpool dockside pub. As a child she had lived among sailors, docks, shipping. She had vivid memories.

The Prince asked again: 'But why Liverpool?'

'They could be planning to get her out of the country,' added Skittles. 'To Ireland.'

This appalling idea produced complete silence. The train was moving backwards at not much more than fifteen miles an hour, and there was little noise from the outside.

'Why do you say that?' asked General Grey.

She put it into words. 'The docks are there. Ships are there. Thousands of Irish are there. Ireland isn't far away . . .'

John Brown, who had his flask and had also found a glass – his instinct was unerring – banged the glass down. 'Over my dead body, only . . .'

The Prince broke in sharply: 'Our concern is with the Queen's *live* body.'

'Hear, hear,' murmured several voices.

'God save us from unplanned rescue attempts,' declared the Prince. 'Ours or anyone else's. We can control our own – I hope. But how about the others? How long before the nation learns what is happening? There are men in every town and village who will stop at nothing. How are they to know that rescue attempts will be her death warrant? How are we to tell them? General Grey, what do you say?'

General Grey, the oldest person present by many years, looked less distraught than the others. His earthly ambitions had been all but fulfilled. He had seen much, and his life's course couldn't, in the nature of things, have much longer to go. The crisis had given him the alertness of a much younger man. But he knew this to be temporary. About a year ago, and he recalled the date exactly – 14 October – he had given the Queen a warning, based on secret reports from Manchester, that the Fenians had designs on her. In that city, five Irishmen had attempted to rescue two Fenian prisoners from a prison-van, and in the fracas a British policeman had been shot and killed. On 23 November – and he remembered *that* date – three of those five would-be rescuers had been hanged. A deputation had attempted to see the Queen to plead for mercy. He, Grey, had seen to it the deputation never reached her. He knew it to be useless anyway. He also knew a black cloud of hate would hover over the Queen.

Aloud, to the Prince, he said: 'Sir, we need three things: Co-ordination. Communication. Imagination. Nothing less will save her.'

'Large words,' responded the Prince.

'All rescue attempts must be co-ordinated with you and have your approval, sir. Communications must be opened and maintained somehow with the government. I would suggest that Knollys direct that part of it. As for imagination, sir, God give us the ingenuity and guile to circumvent these monsters.'

Grey had offered two names. A third was needed. The Prince's gaze moved from face to face. By instinct he lighted on his old friend Chaplin first. Tried, true and honourable. But Harry was incapable of ingenious ideas. He cherished horses, expensive dinners, expensive company and old ideas. General Grey himself – no, he was scarcely an ideas man either, although he had reached high army rank; and he was wise, too. Jenner had better stay with his pills. Then he came to Skittles.

The grey eyes hid the guile underneath so effectively that few suspected its existence. She knew all the tricks; she had imagination. But it would be impossible to bring her to the front. The Queen, he half suspected, might even prefer being blown up to a rescue engineered by Skittles. At any rate, she would find the choice a most painful one.

His gaze travelled to Hartington. He appeared to be yawning slightly, although that seemed scarcely credible. Some fleeting indisposition no doubt. The admirable thing about Hartington was that he never lectured nor offered advice (unless asked) and when he did say anything, which was rarely, he spoke sound common sense. He didn't dissimulate either. He was in love and living openly with the Duchess of Manchester (the Duke was impossible), but, for the moment, he was smitten with Skittles, and they were like a couple of children together.

The Prince had an idea. The way things stood, Skittles and Hartington practically amounted to the same thing. The third man should be Lord Hartington. 'It will be your duty,' the Prince announced, 'to originate and encourage anyone else to originate plans for rescue.' He repeated with emphasis, 'Anyone.'

To the surprise of all, Hartington nodded as though he had somehow anticipated it. And unexpectedly he asked a question. 'How do we know they actually do have gunpowder?'

The Prince looked at Grey.

'They said so,' said Grey. 'The way they acted ... I must say ... actually, no. If you put it to me, I have no positive proof.'

'How can we get proof?' asked the Prince.

'Ask them,' said Hartington. 'I mean to say, we've got to know.'

The train began to bang and creak, a sign that it was slowing down. It came to rest short of Ballinluig station. Directly ahead stretched the way to Stanley Junction and, beyond, to England, while, on the right, the branch line meandered westward to Aberfoyle.

The gong boomed once.

'Come, Hartington,' said the Prince. Brown started to rise too. 'Not you, Brown. Stay where you are. Police officers, keep an eye on him.'

The Prince and the heir to the Duchy of Devonshire marched together to answer Todhunter's summons. He was waiting for them.

'Who's this?' he asked, when he saw Hartington.

The Prince told him, adding, 'friend of mine'.

'Your concern, Your Royal Highness, is to get this train to Liverpool quickly. Where is your railway man?'

'I suspect he's on his way,' replied Hartington, looking down the line with maddening calmness. 'I see him, yes . . . I understand you claim to have gunpowder. How are we to know it's gunpowder?'

Todhunter regarded Hartington as if making sure in his own mind whether he was confronted with a knave or a fool. 'You don't,' he exclaimed finally.

'We therefore have to assume it isn't,' responded Hartington, 'with all that implies.'

Todhunter's mouth tightened ominously, but a pause followed, and it appeared that his confederate inside was conveying a message.

'See for yourself,' said Todhunter finally. 'You only.'

He opened the door. Hartington climbed up. In a minute, he was down again.

'Yes, gunpowder,' he said. And then Gilkes arrived.

The Duke of Cambridge was impatiently perusing the text of the message scribbled by Monty for the Commander of the Forces in Scotland, when there was an interruption.

The door of the Prime Minister's study was flung open to disclose Hale, the amateur telegraphist, with his hair dishevelled. The manners he had acquired as a palace footman seemed to have been abandoned. The Duke's equerry, a captain of Hussars, standing by the door, who was so marvellously attired that he looked like the caricature of an equerry, was taken by surprise. He jerked his monocle from his eye.

Hale looked round the room and spotted Ponsonby. 'Ah, there you are, sir.'

'Who the devil is this?' growled the Duke; but the Prime Minister, by virtue of that sixth sense of his, had already divined what was in the wind, and, rising from his seat, prepared himself for grave news.

'What is it, Hale?' asked Ponsonby.

'Message for him,' answered Hale, pointing at the Prime Minister, and again completely forgetting his training.

'Give it, dammit, give it,' exclaimed the Duke excitedly.

'... Message coming through from the Prince, sir. From Ballin-luig. Desperadoes have seized the Queen ... seized the Queen ...' Hale had reached the stage where he was repeating himself, and was badly shaken.

'By God, we're too late,' exclaimed the Duke, pounding the desk.

'Take me to the telegraph-room,' said the Prime Minister. 'Your Royal Highness, Ponsonby, you may wish to accompany me ...'

Hale led the way. Disraeli followed and the others swarmed after. Monty and the Duke's equerry brought up the rear. They sped downstairs to the cellar level and through dark passages. They heard the clatter of the telegraph instrument before they arrived at the small dark room.

The telegraph operator at Number 11, who had had experience of reporting wars, assassinations, victories, and disasters, and who, before the era of the telegraph, had handled 'most secret' documents arriving by sail, by coach-and-four, and by special couriers on horseback, was a cool customer, quite imperturbable. An oil-lamp provided a hazy light. Although he knew, after a glance over his shoulder, who his sudden visitors were, it made not the slightest difference to him, except that his long thin nose twitched a couple of times.

'Give us what you have got,' said Disraeli.

The operator, whose name was Evans, beckoned to Hale to take his place.

'Who is at the other end of the line now?' asked Disraeli. 'The Prince?'

'Sir John Cowell is now at the other end, sir.'

'Cowell? Cowell?' muttered Disraeli. 'Master of the House-hold as I recall. Very well. Proceed.'

Evans consulted a sheaf of papers. He began:

'This part is from the Prince, sir. His message: "Two conspirators in sergeant-footman's compartment on Queen's coach, with large load of gunpowder, have seized effective control over life and person of Queen. Any attempt at rescue from outside could be instantly fatal. Conspirators have ordered train to Liverpool. Conjecture they may try to remove Queen by ship, possibly to

Ireland. Can do nothing else but comply at this moment. Clearly Fenian plot. Attempts at rescue must be guided only by those of us directly at or near scene. I now leave for Liverpool. Cowell remains. He has instructions. Edward P." '

The Duke sat down heavily in a rickety chair, the only spare one in the place. He was now as shaken as at any time during the Crimean War, when, much to the Queen's annoyance, he had to be shipped home. His bellicosity was only skin deep.

The Prime Minister turned to Monty. 'Convey a message to Euston station. The destination of our train will be Liverpool. Speed is of the essence.'

The Prime Minister turned to Ponsonby. 'Colonel Ponsonby, will you be so good as to proceed from here and take Lord Hastings into custody immediately. This may well tax your diplomatic talents to the fullest. On paper you have authority for nothing. Neither have I. Your Royal Highness, will you permit your equerry to accompany Colonel Ponsonby on this mission? Military assistance may be needed.'

'Eh?' said the Duke. 'Yes, take him. Captain Adair, consider yourself under the Colonel's orders. Temporarily.'

Captain Adair saluted.

'And, Colonel,' the Prime Minister continued, 'I want the person of Lord Hastings delivered to the special train. For interrogation. During the journey. In addition, I want delivered any others involved – any we can lay our hands on ... Who could those be?'

Ponsonby considered: 'McClune, Hastings's agent, first and foremost. Anyone we can find at the McClune household. The Hastings coachman; O'Toole, the former palace telegraphist ...'

The name of Cora crossed his mind, but he omitted her. She was not really a first-hand source and she could be picked up later if needed. Besides, he already had her story. He added, 'Collecting these people will hold up the departure of the train, sir.'

'We will use a second train if necessary, to follow the first,' snapped the Prime Minister. 'Your mission is to bring them in.'

'Then I will need more assistance.'

'You shall have it. I speak for His Royal Highness. Take four of his guardsmen; take a couple of my clerks; take the two police-men attached to Number 10.' The Prime Minister waved a dis-missal and turned to the telegraph machine.

The operator, Evans, stood at attention. 'Continuing the mes-sage, sir. This part is from Sir John Cowell: "I left Balmoral this morning, with small squad to establish emergency telegraphic communications following the cutting of the telegraph line to the castle, as reported earlier. Arriving at Blair Atholl, I learned there that Queen's train was detained at Killiecrankie for reasons un-known" . . .'

'I learned, I learned,' hissed the Duke. 'To the devil with his learning. Get to the heart of it.'

'I believe we are getting to the substance of things now, your Grace,' continued the telegraphist. There was almost the faintest note of reproof in his voice, but as His Royal Highness could not detect a *nuance* unless it was blasted out of a cannon, this did not upset him in any way.

' "Using post horses and leaving the squad behind, I arrived by road near Killiecrankie just in time to see Queen's train start moving backwards along the viaduct, apparently retracing steps to Ballinluig. I was able to ride my horse along footpath on to railway line where I found a second engine commencing to fol-low train. This was pilot engine driven by Earl of Kendal. With him was Gilkes, official of Highland Railway. I abandoned horse and transferred to engine. There learned real situation.

' "When Queen's train drew near to Ballinluig, one of conspira-tors ordered it shunted up branch line and back again, manoeuvre which brought engine to front. Prince's section was ordered de-tached.

' "Gilkes told to move Queen's section to Liverpool forthwith. Route to be: Stanley Junction, Carlisle, Kendal, Lancaster, Pres-ton, Liverpool. Gilkes protested such movement unsafe unless arranged in advance with other railways involved, principally London North Western. Gilkes given ultimatum of ten minutes. Gilkes then stricken with fainting spell or seizure. Fell to ground. Jenner summoned, revived him, at least temporarily. Placed in compartment. No other railway official being available, Ballinluig station-master pressed into service. Is now on Queen's train.

' "Hartington suggested using name of Queen on telegraphic instruction to other railways involved peremptorily declaring her intention of travelling to Liverpool instantly for 'reasons of state'. Prince concurred. I personally dispatched this. Am also personally telegraphing now . . ." '

'What's that?' broke in Disraeli. 'Correct! I had forgotten. He was with the Royal Engineers.'

The operator continued:

' "In addition to collapse of Gilkes, Lady Ely was in fainting condition. She also was removed from train by Dr Jenner. Emile Dittweiler, Queen's dresser, is staying with her. The other dresser, Mary Nolan, now attending Queen.

' "Ten minutes after Queen's train pulled out, Prince ordered Earl of Kendal to connect his engine to Prince's section and follow at distance, out of view. Both sections now bound for Liverpool. I also took liberty of issuing instructions to railways concerning Prince's train. I await orders. Cowell." '

'Can I communicate directly with Cowell?' demanded the Prime Minister.

'Yes, sir.'

'Then send as follows: Your message received. Your services most highly commended. Prime Minister responding directly. Did you see conspirators? Did you recognize them? Have you any clues?'

By telegraph, the following messages were exchanged between Sir John Cowell and the Prime Minister:

'Saw both. Recognize neither. No clues, as yet.'

'Describe them.'

'First man, officer type, black hair. About forty-five. Middle height. Obviously in command, but stays in background. Other looks sinister. Named Todhunter. About six feet two. Thin cheekbones, wide mouth.'

'Have reason to believe officer-type man is McClune, agent of Lord Hastings,' interposed the Prime Minister.

'Would not know. Have learned train from north is due at Blair Atholl. Seek authority to commandeer engine and one coach. Purpose, to follow Queen and Prince using squad in any capacity that may be needed. Two of men are telegraphists.'

'Proposal approved. Use any authority – also caution – necessary. Am myself leaving for Liverpool. How do we maintain touch? Crucial problem.'

'Will leave initial message at Carlisle,' Cowell answered. 'Will check there for message from you. Will repeat procedure at later stations. Goodbye.'

As Sir John Cowell described it later, the crisis of his life was the few minutes spent on the telegraph *after* his conversation with Disraeli. His squad was up at Blair Atholl. He had to reach them before the train arrived from the north, not only to get the men aboard it and down where he was, but he needed them for the business of commandeering.

Commandeering in war is one thing; in peacetime – particularly in Scotland – another. He, Cowell, was not a large, official-looking person with a booming voice. He had no written orders, with or without the Royal Seal. Actually he couldn't even prove who *he* was; he had nothing official on him. His witnesses had gone. The station-master had been taken south as a sort of replacement for the ailing Gilkes. The lone porter was away on an errand of mercy; he was escorting Lady Ely, along with Emile Dittweiler, to Fisher's Hotel, some four miles distant. Only an old Scotch terrier was left to keep him company. No doubt, in time, he could make out a case for the forcible removal of a railway engine which was presumably pulling a train filled with individuals all of whom were anxious to get to places 'without let or hindrance'. But nothing he could do or say would prevent the train staff from verifying everything; and not only might this take hours, it could lead to God knew what complications.

But the crisis passed. The fates were with him. A matter of seconds was involved, and he was able to make contact.

Twenty-five minutes later the train steamed into Ballinluig station. First out was a florid-faced guard who made a beeline for him. 'Are these men yours, sir?' and he pointed to the High-landers piling out of a third-class compartment.

'Why?'

'Why? I ask you, where are their tickets? Not one amongst them.'

'What's the fare?' demanded Sir John. 'Give me the total.' He summoned the sergeant and told him to stand by. The sergeant lined up the men 'at ease'.

While the guard pored over his figures, the passengers began opening doors and peering out of windows. To Sir John's consternation, every single one was a clergyman.

'What the hell have we got here?' he whispered to the sergeant.

'Some sort of excursion for the clergy,' the sergeant replied. 'Ye'll find something in writing on yon window.'

Sir John moved over and discovered the words

'CURATES
CLERICAL
CLUB'

'Twenty-four shillings,' the guard called out, 'and I'll be obliged if you'll step into the station-master's office and fill out the necessary forms.'

'Here's five pounds, and keep the change,' answered Sir John. 'The station-master isn't there. Guard, in the name of Her Majesty the Queen, and on the orders of the Prime Minister, I have to inform you that I am immediately commandeering this engine – the driver, the stoker – and the first coach of this train.'

'You're mad!' exclaimed the guard. He took a tighter hold on the five-pound note, took a quick (and reassuring) look at it, and transferred it to a pocket with magical speed. The clergy were now tumbling out and forming a circle about the Highlanders. A couple of them, white-haired, held up hands, calling for order.

'What is this, sir?' demanded the most venerable of them, who evidently had long since ascended from the ranks of curate. He peered accusingly at Sir John through bushy eyebrows. 'I do not know what this outrage is all about. But I will inform you that I am not without influence; and I have had the privilege of preaching before Her Majesty in person, and . . .'

'I am aware of that,' interjected Sir John. 'I was present and heard you; you are Canon Brewster. For your information, I am the Master of the Royal Household. Take my word for it, only the gravest affair of state brings this about. I call for your assistance in the name of the Queen. I say no more at the moment. All will be clear later. Get everyone off the train.'

The Canon began clucking like a hen.

Sir John turned away and strode to the engine to talk with the driver and stoker who had been absorbed in the drama. They had seen the Highlanders and that was convincing enough. It took only a few minutes to complete the unhitching and to assign one member of the squad to stay behind as a link and a relay-point. That man was a telegraphist. He would begin tapping out an urgent message to railway authorities, drafted while Sir John was waiting:

'For reasons of state, Her Majesty's government has ordered special train to accompany Queen's train, also Prince's train, now *en route* to Liverpool. Special consists of engine, one coach. Highland Railway engine Number 27 [this was inserted later]. All three trains to be treated as sections of Royal train, having right of way at all times. Disraeli.'

The Prime Minister had endorsed direct action, and this was it.

Now Number 27 was ready to take off.

'Sergeant,' Sir John called out, 'put one of your best men on the footplate. You join me in the first compartment. Split the squad between the next two compartments ... I want to arrange some sort of rough communication with the engine. A piece of rope will do. We'll set up a rough code.'

The sergeant peered over the heads of the clergy, milling about forlornly, and spied a piece of line which the station-master evidently used for runner beans in his adjoining garden. He produced a dirk and chopped it off.

'Here you are, sir.' He tied one end of the string to the engine and brought the other through the far window of the compartment. Sir John took it and anchored it. 'My man's the other telegraphist in the squad, sir. He'll have no trouble with any code.'

'Telegraphist!' exclaimed Sir John. 'Tell him to hang on to his end. I'm going to send him a message.'

Using the International Code, he jerked out: 'Your name?'

Back came the answer: 'Drum.'

Sir John jumped on to the platform to take a look at Drum, who turned out to be young James Drum from Inverness. 'You are the watchdog,' he told him. 'Report everything ... All right, Sergeant, we'll get moving.'

The driver of engine Number 27 was far from being a senior on the system, nor was he the conservative type. He was indeed one of the youngest. He had the luxury of pulling just one coach, with all railway rules apparently abandoned. In a few minutes, although he had no means of knowing it, he was already travelling faster than the Queen's train or the Prince's train. The coach rocked wildly, and Cowell blinked at the blast of air coming through the window. The stations of Guay and Dalguise flashed by.

'The devil himself must be up in front,' was the sergeant's comment. 'If he is doing this on a rugged, winding line, what'll he do when we get to the straight stretches?'

Cowell nodded. As the remark sank in, an idea occurred to him. The speed was unusual. If it kept up, could they not catch up with the Queen's train? Perhaps even make a detour round and get ahead of it? It was a possibility. He did not know whether it would be wiser to get ahead or to stay behind, and if he did get ahead, what could he do? It could be a great gamble. His instinct told him to try for it.

A pull on the line brought him back to reality. He signalled an acknowledgment. It was a spotty message because Drum was obviously being tossed around on the footplate. Eventually Sir John made out the words: 'Clergyman with us.'

'Impossible,' snorted Sir John. He leaned out to catch sight of the face and collar of a clergyman peering from the rearmost compartment. Angrily he sent back the message: 'Stop train.'

Brakes began grinding, and he found, when they had finally pulled to a halt, that they were already at Stanley Junction, at the near end of the platform.

Sir John got out.

The sergeant got out.

The clergyman got out.

At the same time a trio of well-dressed gentlemen began moving towards them from the distance.

Sir John confronted the clergyman: 'Why did you not get off the train at Ballinluig, sir? You were requested to do so.'

'My brethren are sheep, I fear,' was the reply. 'I do not happen to be one.'

'What is your name, sir? What explanation have you got for being here?'

'I am the Reverend Charles Anderson, Vicar of St John's, Limehouse, London. I had hoped against hope I could somehow get south in a hurry. An obligation, a personal matter I'll not trouble you with. At least this train seemed to be going in a southerly direction; I ventured to intrude.' The Reverend Anderson had twinkling blue eyes. Sir John thought, why not? The universe is upside down. He may bring us luck.

Aloud he said, 'Very well. You are liable to be ejected at any moment. You understand that? Move into the first compartment, please.' He could keep an eye on him there.

The Vicar of St John's beamed, lifted his humble carpet bag, and made the move. The three newcomers arrived, and Sir John recognized a familiar figure: John Winston Spencer Churchill, seventh Duke of Marlborough. He had side-whiskers and looked like a solicitor or a churchwarden – a striking mutation from previous Marlboroughs. In addition, he was a leader of those who bitterly opposed the opening of art galleries, museums, and libraries on Sunday afternoons for the benefit of the people, not to mention Sunday playing by military bands. He happened to be a member of Disraeli's first cabinet, principally because Disraeli doted on Dukes (he had collected no less than three of them, along with seven other members of the nobility, in a cabinet totalling fourteen) but he was relegated to a comparative sinecure as President of the Council. However, he was doing something to earn his keep, if the phrase could be used in his case, by acting as the

Minister in Attendance at Balmoral. How cabinet members struggled to evade *that* assignment! Cold corridors, dreary meals, boredom generally. If they could escape, they did; and the Duke evidently had managed to get away for a while. And he had missed the drama.

He hoarsely introduced the two other men as railway officials. 'What's this, Cowell? What are these reports? What the devil is happening? The truth, man, the truth!'

Sir John gave him a summary. It took him precious minutes. He concluded: 'Discipline has to be maintained, whatever the cost. A damnable fact, but true.'

'I shall accompany you', declared the Duke.

'Very good, your Grace. My aim is to pass the Queen's train if possible. But we are losing time.' He turned to the railway men. 'Can I do it? And where?'

One, a bearded giant, looked at his watch. 'This side of Carlisle could be the place. There's a detour there. Leave this to us. I am the locomotive superintendent of the line. I am taking over the driving. The driver will act as stoker. The stoker will come along as reserve.'

Number 27 moved out of Stanley Junction. It picked up speed (it was clear the superintendent was every bit as fast as his junior predecessor). The Duke, the clergyman, the Master of the Royal Household, and the sergeant sat in silence.

His Grace was the first to speak: 'I believe it would be appropriate if the vicar would offer a prayer on *her* behalf.'

Vicars are supposed to be more than willing to offer a prayer at the drop of hat. But the Reverend Charles Anderson was not an ordinary vicar. He had a desperately poor parish and his humble church abutted on the Limehouse gasworks. He had an income of £300 a year, out of which he had to pay for the choir and the upkeep of the building, which left him perhaps £2 a week to live on. His parishioners worked fifteen hours a day, six days a week. He had come to doubt the creed of the Church of England, and was seriously depressed. As a result, he couldn't stand another hour of being bottled up with the curates – which was all that his 'obligation' to get south in a hurry amounted to. A white lie? Or a grey lie? He didn't care. Nor did he care about the pious aristocrat sitting opposite him, whom he considered a pious fraud. Thus his response was less than prudent.

'I am willing to do so, your Grace, but if you will permit me to say so, matters are much too serious for that.'

'Too *serious*,' repeated His Grace, who was not sure that he had heard correctly. 'I do not understand you.'

'Putting it bluntly, your Grace, it is a waste of time. What we need is action on earth, here and now.'

The Duke recoiled as though he detected something moving on his plate. 'It was my impression that you were a man of the cloth. Are you not a clergyman of the Church of England? Is not the Queen the head of the Church? Does she not require divine assistance?'

'If you press me, sir, I will have to say I have no better channel leading to divine assistance than has anyone in this compartment. What she needs is *our* assistance. And *yours*, if you happen to have any ideas.'

'Outrageous,' exploded the Duke. 'Cowell, who is this man? I have been misled. I don't want his company.'

'I know nothing about him,' said Sir John, who was having a hard time trying to fit the vicar into any pigeonhole that he recognized. As far as he was concerned, clergymen acted by rote in a certain way and if they didn't something was wrong. 'I suppose you could call him a stowaway. He was at a curates' conference.' He turned to the culprit. 'We had better drop you as soon as possible.' Something in the clergyman's eye – and he was to ruminate over this later – caught his attention. 'Or put you in the rear compartment. Take your choice.'

'I apologize,' said the vicar. 'I fear I am ahead of my time.' He raised his hand slowly in a compelling gesture, as though he were on the stage, and it was evident he was quite an actor. 'I have a vision of a Church and the laws of our land that will not seek to stop, but will *encourage*, the enrichment of the mind on the Sabbath.'

'Heresy,' thundered the Duke. 'The Sabbath is set aside for the enrichment of the soul, not the mind. The sanctification of the

Sabbath will bring abundant reward. Remember His words: "Them that honour Me, I will honour".'

The vicar appeared unmoved. He seemed to be talking to no one in particular. He said: ' "The hungry sheep look up and are not fed": Milton.'

Number 27 pounded on.

6

When Colonel Ponsonby left the Prime Minister at Downing Street, his first task was, if possible, to seize the Marquis of Hastings, along with anyone who might be able to shed light on anything – a category which included Joe, the coachman, and anybody else who might be picked up at the McClune residence.

Ponsonby was now speeding in a carriage to 34 Grosvenor Square, the London home of the Marquis, while another carriage, with two policemen in it, was following unobtrusively. With him was Captain Adair, equerry to the Commander-in-Chief.

Another search-party was out looking for O'Toole, the dismissed palace telegraphist.

Captain Adair was not given to conversation. When he did speak, it was in monosyllables with an exaggerated accent, and with the lisp cultivated by cavalry officers. Ponsonby judged him to be about twenty-three, which was his own age when he first became a captain in the Grenadier Guards. He was glad of the silence. The events of the day unravelled in his mind in shot-gun fashion, and were unaccountably intermingled with recollections from long ago, no doubt because he was in a strange mental state. For some reason and quite vividly, he saw himself back in the trenches in the Crimea. It was an August night. The trenches were only three feet deep, too low to be of any use, and the ground was white limestone and chalk. A Russian shot hit the parapet near him and the impact knocked him down. He wasn't hurt much, but when he got back to friendly surroundings, covered with chalk, and white and ghost-like in the moonlight, the impact on his friends was memorable.

When they reached Grosvenor Square, the trooper leaped down from the box.

'Stand by,' said Ponsonby.

With Adair standing beside him he pulled the bell. A footman answered. 'Kindly tell His Lordship that I have an urgent message from the Prime Minister, and must see him immediately,' said Ponsonby, who had given a great deal of thought to just what he would say and how. He had decided it would be a waste of time to stand on the niceties of social custom.

The footman for once forgot his training and looked slightly startled. The captain in his Hussar uniform, with swaying sword and glamorous fur cap with a green plume, somehow conveyed an air of indolent menace. He also looked foreign; since the uniform had simply been copied outright from the Hungarians, this was not unexpected. Ponsonby, when the occasion called for it, could always look like an English version of the Inspector-General – which he was now doing; and in the background were the two guardsmen.

The two men were invited to enter. They stood in a dim entrance hall. A butler arrived on the scene and they watched the footman hold a nervous conversation with him.

The butler disappeared. When he returned, who should be with them but Lady Hastings. She came forward, walking lightly – gliding perhaps would be a more accurate description – a tiny, fetching figure, and Captain Adair was able to summon up enough energy to elevate his monocle, and this time to leave it in place.

Colonel Ponsonby introduced himself. 'Equerry to Her Majesty, ma'am.' The captain clicked his heels. Ponsonby added, 'I have a message of the gravest importance for Lord Hastings's ears alone, please.'

Lady Hastings bit her lip. When the butler had come to her with news of the visitation, she felt at once that her worst fears were being realized. It had only been a matter of a few hours ago, so it seemed, that her warning letter had been delivered to Chaplin.

How she had hated sending that! It had been a betrayal, yes; but the motive had been good, she felt sure.

She said, 'You realize, Colonel, that Lord Hastings is ill – seriously ill, I fear.'

'I regret to hear it, ma'am. But this business will not wait.'

She led them along a corridor to a small side-room that adjoined a larger dining-room. His Lordship, pale, with a badly trimmed beard, was wearing a silk dressing-gown over at least part of his day clothes, and was toying with a snack, which appeared, from pungent evidence, to consist of mackerel fried in gin.

The two men remained standing. 'Kindly leave us, ma'am,' said Ponsonby.

'Stay where you are, Florence,' said the Marquis. 'What is all this about? By the way, Colonel, who are *you* to tell my wife to leave? I understand the bailiffs may be interested in me, but this is still my house.'

'I had hoped to save her embarrassment,' answered Ponsonby. 'What this visit is about is High Treason.' He let the dread words sink in.

The Marquis briefly halted the progress of a piece of mackerel to his mouth, and then consumed it calmly. He had struggled hard to maintain composure all his life, but, unlike his rival Chaplin, who oozed poise from every pore and on all occasions, it never really came naturally. 'Most interestin'. May I inquire the details? Am I bein' arrested?'

'The details, which will have to suffice for the moment, are that the Queen is in the gravest danger. There is evidence that you are implicated. You are not under arrest. That is a technicality. Not to put too fine a point on it, you are being seized. I am requesting you to accompany us – instantly. You are to be taken to Euston station, put aboard a special train, and interrogated by the Prime Minister.'

'And you propose to do this, to a peer of the realm? Without the slightest legal basis?'

'Not *propose* to do so. To do. Come with me, sir, as you are now.'

'Are you telling me I cannot even put a coat on?'

'Put a coat on, if you have one handy.'

Lady Hastings left the room. She returned with a frockcoat and helped the Marquis make the exchange; she faced Ponsonby. 'You, sir, be my witness. This is a horrible error. Believe me, I know. You must believe *me*. And my husband is in no condition to be taken away. Can't you see that?'

'I commiserate with you, madam. No innocent party will suffer, let me assure you. There is a member of your household staff we will take with us. Your coachman, Joe.'

Florence exchanged some hurried words with the butler, and holding her husband's arm solicitously moved out to the street and entered the carriage. Joe emerged from a side entrance and took his place on the box without a word, except that he mumbled as he touched his hat to Ponsonby, a gesture that conveyed much.

As they moved off, Florence dabbed a tear from her eye. Four years had gone by since, as the 'Pocket Venus', she had been the rage and toast of society, and had fled from Chaplin into the arms of Hastings. Her enemies had said it was because Hastings had a better title and was a better match. The truth was that she had never really loved Chaplin and had told him so. He was kind. good, dull, quite pompous, and, as far as she was concerned, just 'dear old Harry'.

Now, alas, his kindness, and even his dullness, seemed attractive. Since her wedding-day, her disillusionment had been progressive. And to cap it all, a charge of High Treason! She began to cry without restraint. There seemed to be no hope and no reprieve.

A phrase kept running through Ponsonby's mind as he saw the tears running down the cheeks of Lady Hastings: 'When lovely woman stoops to folly.' She had been a Paget before her marriage, and the Pagets had a wild history. He directed the driver to go up Baker Street, and, when they reached the McClune home, he ordered a division of forces.

Captain Adair would hurry with Hastings on to Euston. He (Ponsonby) would use the second carriage, as well as the services of the two policemen. He would handle the McClune situation.

He rapped sharply on the knocker. The woman who opened

the door was the same he had seen earlier. Thin-faced. This time she had her arms folded.

'Does Captain McClune live here?' he asked.

'When he's in London, yes.'

'Is he in?'

'No.'

'Where is he, please?'

'I have no idea.' She was about to shut the door when Ponsonby put his foot in it. The policeman pushed his way past. Ponsonby followed. They were in a corridor.

'Get out, get out,' shouted the woman.

'This is a serious police matter,' said Ponsonby, with his usual gravity. 'No use protesting. You won't be harmed. Where are McClune's rooms?'

'What right have you to come in? Where's your warrant? What are you up to?'

'Looks like his rooms are here,' came the voice of the policeman from a doorway. He was surveying a living-room which was empty of all those knick-knacks and ornaments which are an extension of individual taste. The furniture, polished to mirror brightness, looked as though it ought to be in a shop window. Someone had gone over the place with a brush, water, wax, and a cloth. The cupboard was bare. The bird had flown.

Outside, one of the horses whinnied. Ponsonby scrutinized his watch. 'What is your name, madam?'

'That's my business.'

'Do you live here?'

'Yes.'

'Where?'

'Downstairs.'

Ponsonby considered the time element. He could delay no longer.

'Madam, I'm compelled to ask you to accompany me to be interrogated.' He preferred persuasion if it would work. But the woman was belligerent.

'I won't.'

The policeman gave Ponsonby a knowing look. 'We can handle

this very nicely, I think, sir. I know the type.' He smiled as though about the enjoy himself and went to the front door to alert his colleague, standing by the carriage.

The woman crept into a corner and remained immobile against the walls.

'There isn't any way out of it,' said Ponsonby. 'Put your coat on and come.'

She simply stared at him.

The policeman returned, full of false breeziness. 'All right, my good woman, we'll be as gentle as we can, ha, ha, but you're coming ...' He grabbed her arm, twisted it behind her, bent her double, and marched her outside. When she reached the carriage she fell down. The other policeman lifted her in like a sack of coal.

She will need a coat, thought Ponsonby. At the end of the corridor, he saw the stairs to the basement. He made the descent as quickly as he dared. There was a room to his left. A kettle was singing on a stove; he turned off the burner. On the table was a small pile of newspapers, and he caught sight of the word *Daily Post*. A family portrait of some sort hung on the wall ... The coat, at any rate *a* coat, he found in a cupboard.

As he hurried to the street he was already reaching a decision. 'Officer,' he said to the policeman, 'I want every piece of paper, writing, book, magazine, newspaper, photograph, calendar, and the pictures off the wall in that room. I want them collected now and brought to me at Euston station. Here's a sovereign. Use it for a cab when you are through. As fast as you can.'

He climbed into the carriage, facing the woman and the other policeman. Her coat was over his arm. She looked at it without comment.

He could not account for her actions. Why the vehemence? What was behind it? Or was she merely defending her rights?

No greater contrast could be imagined than the white face of Disraeli alongside the bulbous nose of the Duke of Cambridge, as they shared a carriage *en route* to Euston station. The Duke was petulant, frustrated. His code was a simple one involving two words: 'charge' and 'retreat'. Unfortunately, neither could be bent to cope with the present situation.

Disraeli, for his part, was reflective. As the carriage turned through the granite Greek arch of the huge new structure, he was looking back to his own youth when there were no railway stations. Now, or so someone had told him, there were more than 4,500 in the country, and the number was growing each month. The railway was transforming the English way of life. It was ironic that an instrument of such promise should be used to abduct the Queen.

The carriage came to a stop and the Duke (of course) descended first. A group of officials was waiting and they were escorted into a large room evidently used by the railway directors.

The London and North Western Railway was a powerful company. Its lines linked London, Liverpool, and the north. The men at the top of LNWR were imbued with an overriding obsession: *dividends*. One manager even had the word DIVIDENDS in large letters pasted on his window – a perpetual reminder, and a variation from those other texts so plentifully scattered far and wide: 'God Bless our Home' and 'God is Love'.

A Yorkshireman, by the name of Edgar Thurloe, was the first to speak. He was the managing director. 'I'll not try and pull wool over your eyes, sir. We have become aware of what's been on the telegraph. Not all of it. But enough. We know there's wicked business going on. It started at Killiecrankie. The railways own the telegraph lines as you know, sir. Generally speaking, messages are secret. Not in this case.'

This was language the Prime Minister understood. He couldn't blame Thurloe. Next year the telegraph system was to be taken over by the government. But this was *this* year. 'Well, what can you tell *me*?' he asked.

'You are aware, sir, that three trains are presently bound for Liverpool?'

'Yes. Where are they?'

'At the latest report, close to Carlisle. We are informed that the third train will attempt to pass the other two.'

'I did not know that. Sir John Cowell's train?'

'Yes.'

Disraeli surveyed the group facing him. A new plateau had been reached, that was clear. These railwaymen knew almost as much as he did, and it followed that the knowledge was rapidly being spread about. The danger of uncontrolled rescue attempts was increasing. Such attempts might be direct, or indirect, such as blocking the path of the Queen's train, or marooning it up a siding. Or misdirecting it to some other place than Liverpool. It would take only a handful of determined men, at any point along the way, to disrupt the signal system, or to interfere with the engine while it was taking on coal or water.

The Prime Minister had intended to deliver the briefest peroration to the group, calling for discipline, etc., etc. Instead, he reversed his tactics. He told his audience exactly how matters stood, and made no appeals and drew no lessons. The effect, as he anticipated, was profound.

Thurloe spoke up: 'Discipline and deception must be the order of the day, I gather, sir,' almost echoing the words spoken by General Grey to the Prince many miles away, and by Sir John Cowell at Stanley Junction.

'You have stated it in masterly fashion, Mr Thurloe.'

'We will do our part, Mr Prime Minister. Speaking of deception, sir, your train is conspicuous. It has two engines and a number of special coaches. It isn't running on a schedule. A little camouflage would help.'

'What sort of camouflage?'

'Well, sir, we have a train on platform 3 about to be used by the Theatre Arts Society. There are signs on the windows, and some posters. We will transfer these. Your party will become the Theatre Arts Society.'

Disraeli began moving out on to the platform.

'We have added another coach,' Thurloe went on. 'A dozen picked railwaymen will be aboard, and three telegraphists. And a railway doctor. Your own accommodations, sir, are the finest in the country. A model of what Her Majesty, God bless her, is to have next year. We have been testing it.'

It was, in fact, two coaches joined, so it seemed, by a pair of bellows. 'Never been used before ... six wheels apiece. Each unit thirty feet long.'

The Prime Minister viewed this monster quizzically, even with admiration. 'I would like you to join my official party, Mr Thurloe,' he said.

Mr Thurloe had been pondering what he would say if such an invitation came. Could a railway command post function better at Euston or on a moving train, alongside the Prime Minister? A nice question, to which no one could know an answer. He preferred the train himself and said so. 'Very good, sir.'

Further talk was halted when a barrier, which had been set up at the end of the platform, opened. What looked like a batch of carriages was coming through. First, Adair with Lord and Lady Hastings and Joe, the coachman. Ponsonby followed, with the landlady. The policeman was next in a hansom cab. Slung over his shoulder was a load of material wrapped in a sheet. A couple of minutes passed, and a fourth vehicle arrived. O'Toole had been found, but the famous O'Toole grin was missing. All had made it in time, and, although there had been talk of a second train, this wasn't now necessary.

Then a fifth vehicle arrived. It contained a newcomer. It was Lord Cairns, the Lord Chancellor, the sole member of the cabinet that Disraeli's secretary had been able to reach on almost instant notice. He represented the law in its most august aspect, and he was a member of the Privy Council. The Prime Minister now had a colleague whom he could consult. Unfortunately his *real* consultant, Monty Corry, was staying behind.

The Euston station clock showed 4.55 pm.

The Theatre Arts Society special was rushing northwards. The strange human cargo was beginning a strange journey.

The Duke of Cambridge had never travelled anywhere without a different toothbrush for each day. His host could always anticipate the length of his stay by counting his toothbrushes. He was now bound north with none; his batman had somehow failed to get to Euston on time. The Duke's frustrations were almost insupportable, and, in order to recover, he was seeking solace in sleep on a sofa in a small compartment at one end of the coach.

The Prime Minister, heavy-lidded, regarded the flying scenery. He beckoned to the attendant.

'How fast are we travelling?'

The attendant went to a corner and appeared to press a button or pull a switch on a piece of apparatus which was concealed in a small cabinet. When he returned he said, 'Close to fifty miles an hour, sir.'

'How do you know? How did you find that out?'

'This train is equipped with Mr Martin's system of electric communication, sir. I got in touch with the engine.'

'How?' continued the Prime Minister.

'The instrument produces signals in the engine cab, sir, or so I have been informed. Similar to the telegraph. We use the code number 3 to request the speed of the train. I communicated a 3. In return I received a 5, signifying fifty. No doubt, Mr Sinclair himself sent it.'

'Who is Mr Sinclair?'

'Chief engineer of the line, sir. He is on the footplate.'

'Is this system unique to this train?'

'I would have no way of knowing that, sir. One of the officials would have to answer that.'

The Prime Minister nodded, and made a mental note of it ... Did the Queen's train have any such system? If so, would she know about it? Probably not. If she did she would have had it removed; she was opposed to innovation!

The Prime Minister was in the front part of the two-section coach, seated at a table, with Ponsonby on one side, examining the material brought from McClune's rooms, and Lord Cairns on the other. His Lordship was a diffident sort, and not in good health; but he could be a terror when he wanted to. This was the man, the Prime Minister suddenly recalled, who had appeared in some legal capacity (he forgot which) in the famous Windham lunacy case a few years previously. Part of the evidence – of lunacy – alleged that Windham had a craving to drive railway engines, and did so whenever he could get aboard one. In his schooldays (Eton, of course) he had made his mark by running round the school grounds imitating a locomotive, with a lamp in his hand.

The jury found him to be of sound mind.

The Prime Minister's ruminations took an even gloomier turn. What good could come of this chase? How could plans be laid without time for planning? What were the real facts? Why should his happen in *his* term of high office, his first?

He stirred. 'Bring in Lord Hastings,' he ordered.

Captain Adair walked gingerly through the bellows arrangement joining the rocking coaches to the rear of the second section, where the prisoners were assembled, a mixed bag indeed, ranging from the Marquis and Lady Hastings to O'Toole, the sullen telegraphist, Joe, the coachman, and the nameless landlady. Up in front, in a small semi-partitioned compartment, sat Thurloe and one of his railway assistants.

When the Captain returned with the Marquis, he was accompanied by a policeman. The Marquis was directed to take a seat. The Prime Minister concentrated on the young man sitting before him. A beard half hid the weak, amiable face; the pallor was ghastly; the hands shook. He had been brought up by governesses and tutors, grooms, and servants (with some supposed direction by a remote trustee) after his widowed mother had plunged into a life of pleasure and travel. Even when he played cricket at the family seat, Donington Hall, the games were rigged to let him score a run or two; a guinea here and there did the trick.

'Do you know who these men are?' asked the Prime Minister, indicating his companions at the table. 'You do, of course. You may be assured your rights will be preserved.'

'I regret to see the Lord Chancellor lending countenance to this outrage,' replied Hastings. 'His high office won't save him.' He stared at Disraeli. 'Nor will yours.'

The Prime Minister ignored this.

'Do you know where the Queen is now?' he asked.

'Balmoral, I had assumed. I gather I am mistaken.'

'Do you know where the Prince is?'

'I understand he left Euston on a train with Mr Chaplin and Lord Hartington yesterday. No doubt I am mistaken about that, too.'

'Who informed you of the Prince's movements?'

'My agent had informed me. I am not aware there is anything secret about the Prince's movements. There never has been.'

'Your agent is Captain McClune?'

'Yes.'

'And what was your interest in the train?'

'I planned a joke.'

'What sort of joke?'

'It may not sound amusing now but it sounded devilishly amusing at the time. I intended to have some grease put on the railway lines, preferably at some inaccessible point.'

'You personally?'

'Of course not.'

'Who?'

'I left that to McClune.'

'Who was to obtain the grease?'

'McClune.'

'And to apply it?'

'I left that entirely to McClune.'

'And who selected the site?'

'McClune.'

'McClune is the culprit then?'

'McClune is guilty of carrying out a joke if that is what you are getting at. Colonel Ponsonby referred to High Treason. What is the connection?'

'The connection, Lord Hastings, is that *your* joke has been used by *your* agent to seize the person of the Queen, who is a prisoner, who is in grave danger of her life ... At least we have good reason to believe your agent is responsible. Have the goodness to tell us what he looks like.'

Hastings's lips turned white. There was a long pause. 'This is so?' is what finally came out.

'It is.'

Hastings brushed his hand through his hair, a gesture of utter weariness. 'McClune is middle-aged. Black hair ... clean-shaven ...'

'Would you describe him as an officer type?'

'That would be a fair description.'

The Lord Chancellor spoke for the first time, in his high-pitched voice: 'I point out to Lord Hastings what he already knows. In such a crime as this, the law does not admit a separation between Lord Hastings and his agent. The two are indistinguishable. Both are conspirators.'

Hastings said nothing. From the corridor his wife, white of face, emerged, moving slowly towards the table. She took a stand behind him. No one seemed to notice her.

'What do you know about McClune? How long has he been with you?' continued the Lord Chancellor.

'Since I was at Eton.'

'What are his responsibilities?'

'The widest. Practically everything. Management of the tenants, leases ...'

'And your horses?'

'No. I have a trainer for them.'

'Who are McClune's friends and associates?'

'I have no idea.'

'Is he married?'

'He lives as a single man. I am unfamiliar with his history.'

'Did he ever mention relatives or associates?'

'No.'

'What was your degree of curiosity about this?'

'None.'

'Come, sir, you will have to do better than this. Here is a man who has been running the family estates since you were a boy. You tell us you know *nothing* about him? You have not *one single item* of information to contribute?'

Hastings shook his head. He had nothing to offer. In his world there had been only Hastings. He saw that now, but he wasn't going to admit it; it was too late.

'Take him away for the time being, Lady Hastings,' said Disraeli. 'I hope – for his sake – you can refresh his memory.' He doubted, however, whether there was anything to refresh. Hastings seemed to him to be a dying man. He watched the two of them moving slowly down the aisle, like a couple of old people, although neither was yet thirty. Next, he was conscious of Ponsonby leaving his place and coming towards him. He was bending low, and he heard him say: 'The next two witnesses are hostile, sir.'

They held a conference round the table. It was the Lord Chancellor who needed to be briefed, and he nodded in appreciation of Ponsonby's succinct yet balanced recital.

'Bring them in together,' was his decision.

When the couple entered they came shuffling forward, trying to steady themselves against the motion of the train, the woman defiant, O'Toole with bowed head. They sat down.

'The woman first,' barked the Lord Chancellor, who had shed his diffidence. 'What is your name?'

There was no response.

'If I correctly interpret the mood prevailing in this coach, at this minute, you may well be subject to execution out of hand. The crime is High Treason. Think well on it. You are aware your name is a matter of record. You receive letters, do you not? You were born, were you not? There are records, are there not? You have relatives, friends, neighbours? What is your name?'

'Larkin.'

'Miss or Mrs?'

'Mrs.'

'Where is your husband?'

'Dead.'

'Where were you born?'

'Manchester.'

'How long have you known McClune?'

'I don't remember.'

'How did you meet him?'

'I don't remember.'

'We will find means to refresh your memory. Do you own the

premises at Baker Street? There are the records, I remind you.'

'No.'

'Who does?'

'Captain McClune.'

'When did you see him last?'

'I don't remember.'

'Where did he say he was going?'

'He didn't.'

'You saw O'Toole yesterday?'

'Yes.'

'Why?'

'Captain McClune left an envelope for him.'

'And why was that?'

'I don't know.'

'You don't know, or is it inconvenient to remember?'

'I don't know.'

'Had O'Toole been there before?'

'No.'

'Proceed with the questioning, Colonel Ponsonby, while I reflect on the attitude of this witness.'

The Colonel, who had been immersed in quite a mass of papers and correspondence, remained seated. Mrs Larkin puzzled him even more than she had done earlier. She was a housekeeper, but she did not seem the type. He held up several letters. 'Are these yours?'

'I suppose so. You took them.'

'Some are addressed to "Dear Tim". Who is "Dear Tim"?'

'I don't know.'

'Mrs Larkin, you play games with us at your peril,' the Prime Minister interjected. 'McClune's name is Timothy. We know that. You know it.'

Ponsonby waited for her answer, but none came. He continued:

'What were you doing with his letters?'

'He asked me to get rid of them.'

'But you hadn't done so?'

'I was going to.'

'Several of these letters are signed "Aunty". Who is Aunty"?'

Mrs Larkin shook her head.

'... And there are references in the letter signed "Aunty" to "Phoebe". Who is "Phoebe"?'

Another shake of the head.

Ponsonby reached for one of the newspapers that he had spied in her room during his brief visit. He had a moment's shy reflection. The motive for his visit to that room had been kindness, nothing more nor less. He thought she ought to have a coat for a long journey. Perhaps he had been a little ashamed of the seizure and had wanted somehow to offset it. Now, he felt sure, it had been a fateful visit. He held up one of the newspapers.

'This was in your room. Is it yours?'

'No.'

'Whose?'

'I don't know.'

'This newspaper is the *Liverpool Daily Post*. There were six different issues in your room, all recent ...'

The Prime Minister gestured an interruption. 'Hold a minute, Colonel ... Let me see those newspapers ... What have you in mind ...?'

'Something I noticed only a few moments ago,' answered the Colonel, solemnly. 'This!' He pointed to the 'Shipping' column. 'I draw your attention to this marked paragraph ... to the reference to the steamship *Phoebe* ...'

'Let me see the letters, too,' said the Prime Minister. He scrutinized the letters and the marked paper; the Lord Chancellor and the Duke leaned over his shoulder. He read aloud: 'The steamship *Phoebe* is the latest arrival at George's Dock.' He read from the letters: '*Phoebe* will be with us shortly ... All arrangements made for *Phoebe* ...'

It was the Lord Chancellor who responded first:

'Well?'

'I know nothing.'

The Lord Chancellor had the face of a 'hanging judge', and, even without his robes of office, he looked as though he might be posing for an Elizabethan artist, with the Tower of London and the execution block in the background.

He pointed a finger at Mrs Larkin: 'Ah, you *will* speak, you *will* speak,' and to the policeman he added, 'Guard that woman with your life.' He turned to O'Toole:

'And you?'

It was clear all the starch had gone out of O'Toole. He was terrified. 'I had no idea about any of this, your Lordship. No idea at all. I swear it!'

'That we will find out,' said the Lord Chancellor, as he resumed his seat. 'You were in McClune's pay?'

'Not in his pay, my Lord. He gave me a little money for information.'

'What information?'

'He was interested in royal trains.'

'In the Queen's movements? In the Prince's movements?'

'Yes, my Lord.'

'And what was your price for betraying Her Majesty's trust?'

'Ten pounds, my Lord. But I didn't look on it as a betrayal. I was letting him have a little prior information. Not secret information. Just train times.'

'You quibble, O'Toole, and you know it. What has he done with the prior information? What has been the outcome of it? There is your answer . . . What were the circumstances of your meeting with McClune? Where? When?'

'At Mott's, your Lordship. A night establishment. About three months ago, as I remember it.'

'And what drew *you* to him, and McClune to you?'

'A lot of us in the telegraphic business used to go there, my Lord. Still do. Regular clearing house, you might say.'

'A clearing house for what? For confidential information that should not be divulged? For the sale of such information?'

'A harsh way to put it, my Lord. I confess that is so.'

'And how would McClune know that *you* might have what *he* wanted?'

'He made it known, my Lord. I got tipped off what he was

in the market for. Regular exchange going on at Mott's, as I said.'

Nothing further was elicited from O'Toole. The next witness was Joe, who entered wearing his coachman's hat, with its gold cockade, and a heavy coat. He carried his whip in his right hand, as though it were a talisman, which for him it was.

'Colonel Ponsonby,' said Disraeli, 'I understand this is a friendly witness. You have had some connection with him. Proceed, will you?'

'Very well, sir.' The Colonel surveyed the odd character he had wined and dined with, in company with Cora, the previous evening.

'Your full name? You may take off your hat.'

'Joe Belcher, sir, coachman to the Marquis of Hastings. Don't mind if I do take off me 'at.' Joe placed it reverently on the table and, after some hesitation, laid down his whip on the floor, also with reverence.

'How long have you known McClune?'

'About ten years, sir. Cool customer. Oh, very cool.'

'What do you mean by that?'

'Always kept to hisself. Life a closed book. Went to such lengths – never even had his letters delivered at the estate. Had 'em all delivered at his Baker Street place ... Can't really blame the Markis for not knowing what was going on.'

The Lord Chancellor interrupted. 'You have not been called on for your opinions. Keep to the facts.'

'Very good, m'Lord. Just a passing observation.'

'How did you come to know about his letters?' continued Ponsonby.

'It was like this, sir. I'd pick up McClune at Baker Street off and on. Seen the letters there misself. The landlady, or whatever she is, seemed to take charge of them. Her room was downstairs and that's where I'd be.'

'And why would you be *there* rather than in McClune's room?'

'That's where I was told to wait, sir. Downstairs. I never got a foot inside McClune's room.'

'The housekeeper did not object?'

'No, and come to think of it, I couldn't tell what was back of her mind any more 'an I could McClune's. A close one, she was.'

'So you waited. Did you converse with her?'

'Mostly when I waited she wasn't there.'

'Where was she?'

'Judging by the footsteps, upstairs in 'is room, overhead.'

'You would describe the pair as friendly?'

'Oh, very, very.'

'How long were these waits in Mrs Larkin's room?'

'Some ran to 'alf an hour and more, sir. I'd brew misself a cup o' tea. Then I got into the 'abit of throwing a dart or two – without 'er knowing it, o' course.'

'A dart or two?'

'Carry me own darts, sir, and stick the end in a cork for safety. Excellent weapons. As you know, I'm by way of being an expert on rats. I say if you can hit a rat with a dart, you have a sporting proposition. I keep in practice when I can, so I was there throwing darts at spots on the wallpaper, cushions, a picture on the wall – a ship, an' suchlike.'

Ponsonby suffered throughout this irrelevant monologue. The reference to a picture of a ship caught his attention. He had been in the Larkin room only a few hours previously and he felt sure his eye had registered every item.

'A picture of a ship?' he repeated. He flipped through the pile of material he had been examining. The only picture was some sort of family portrait, which was without glass. He held it up. 'Not this?'

Joe shook his head. 'No, sir. Same kind of frame, though.' Joe took a closer look. 'That's strange, sir. There's me dart mark. I hit the frame in the top right-'and corner.'

It was Ponsonby's turn to examine it. Sure enough, there was the small dark hole, where Joe said it should be. He turned over the picture and found, pasted on the back, a rough cover of newspaper. He cut it away. Underneath, and visible from the front, was the family portrait all right, but beneath *that* was something else. He pulled it out into the light of day.

'That's the one,' exclaimed Joe.

It was a coloured lithograph of a ship with two funnels and paddle-wheels. There was a brief legend at the bottom in small print:

'Steamship *Phoebe*. Dimensions: 250 × 30 feet. Tonnage: 1,200. Horsepower: 350. Built by Robert Napier & Sons, Glasgow, for the Cork Shipping Company.'

Ponsonby stared at the vessel, wholly absorbed. There were even a couple of seagulls flying around the bow. The Prime Minister held out an impatient hand. He scrutinized the picture minutely. Eventually he said: 'I infer what we all infer. We have the reason for taking her to Liverpool. They are going to take her aboard this ship.'

'Your death warrant, Mrs Larkin,' hissed the Lord Chancellor.

Mrs Larkin appeared to be shaken by some overwhelming emotion. She spoke convulsively: 'Kill me and have done with it! I don't care. You killed *him*!'

'Him?' enquired the Prime Minister.

'I've said enough.'

'We will be the judge of that – later. Captain Adair, have her taken to the rear, and put her in handcuffs. Leg-irons if necessary ... Ask Thurloe to come here immediately ... Gentlemen, we have to learn everything we can about the *Phoebe*. A waste of breath to say so ... Above and beyond is the question: who can we turn to in Liverpool? Who can pursue enquiries with speed and discretion? Who has the stature, power; who can take command?'

What was uppermost in his mind was the military problem. Events had moved too rapidly for any sort of call to arms through formal channels. Such a call in any event would be self-defeating. It would create an uproar. Even though the Ducal Commander-in-Chief was temporarily immobilised in the arms of Morpheus – and at that moment a grunting noise emerged from the hidden bunk on which he reclined – there were bumblers all around in the upper reaches of the Army. The clique of septuagenarian generals at the Horse Guards, if they ever got the signal, would proceed with the maximum amount of clumsiness, just as, half a century ago, they had attempted to hobble Wellington.

He offered the answer to his own question. 'I think of Stanley. He is now at Knowsley.'

Ponsonby and Cairns exchanged a glance. There could be no better choice. Lord Stanley was Disraeli's Foreign Secretary, and was heir to the vast estates of the elderly and declining Earl of Derby (whom Disraeli had succeeded as Prime Minister), who was now afflicted with gout and the other ailments which had forced his retirement.

The family residence, Knowsley, one of many, was surrounded by 21,000 acres. Not only did these abut on Liverpool, but trains coming from the north passed through or close by the Knowsley estates. Throughout the region the Stanleys were *the* ruling family. Stanleys had been mayors of Liverpool as far back as the sixteenth century. The clan was so grand and ancient that beside it the Cecils seemed like newcomers.

'I detect that you agree with me,' the Prime Minister continued. 'Mr Thurloe, how quickly can we send messages from this train?'

'At any station, sir,' replied Thurloe. 'The train can be slowed down, the message dropped on the platform. It will be picked up and dispatched instantly. All this has been arranged. Or we can slow down sufficiently to drop off our own telegraphist along with the message.'

'Good. Pen, paper, ink . . .' The Prime Minister began to write rapidly. To Monty . . . To Sir John Cowell. 'These will do to start with.' Thurloe handed them to his assistant. 'The most important I leave until last. Mr Thurloe, what I say to Lord Stanley will be vital. It will divulge all. It will be seen by many persons. It is going to the heart of enemy territory – Liverpool. What have you to suggest?'

'Only code will be safe, sir.'

'There is no time for code.'

'I might suggest Latin, sir,' put in Ponsonby, in that mild voice of his.

'By God, that's an idea, Ponsonby. It should give us an hour or two's leeway at least.' Disraeli recalled that the Earl of Derby was an eminent classical scholar. There was no doubt that the son, Lord Stanley, would be at home with Latin.

Latin it should be.

The Prime Minister had called for a respite and was sitting at the table, with his hat tilted over his brow and his arms folded, as though he were in a deep sleep. It was a posture he often adopted in the House of Commons, and in earlier days it had fooled the unwary. It fooled no one now.

He spoke softly, out of the corner of his mouth, to Ponsonby. 'Ponsonby, you recall Mrs Larkin's phrase: "You killed him" ... What did she mean by that?'

'I've been wondering, sir.'

'I have been using my powers of deduction, such as they are. I've been dwelling on Manchester. I have a theory. Either that or a premonition. Will you be so kind as to draft another message. Thank you. This to Monty. As follows: "Immediately telegraph names of three men executed last year for murder of a Manchester policeman. Disraeli."

'... Not altogether a happy case, Ponsonby. It was a rescue attempt. Fenians were being taken to jail in a prison van. One of the rescuers tried to shoot the lock off and killed a policeman. Quite unintentional, I believe. All three of the rescuers were condemned to death. The law is the law ...' A little later, Disraeli made a few notes on a sheet of paper.

'Conspirators – How did they get into sergeant-
footman's compartment? When? Where?
Traitor in the Household? Who?
Dressers – Emile Dittweiler
          Mary Nolan'

After these two names he placed a question mark.

7

The telegraph message that arrived at a small Lancashire railway station outside Liverpool, the one nearest Knowsley Hall, was unlike any other that had been seen there. It appeared to be in code, or in some foreign language. The beginning words, however, were in plain English, and there was no mistaking their meaning. The message was for Lord Stanley. 'Most Urgent. Secret. Deliver with all speed.' And there was a chilling addition from Thurloe no less (who was a Voice on High to LNWR employees): 'Station-master personally responsible.' When the transmission ended, a magic name appeared, 'Disraeli'.

The station-master, a Mr Beech, born and bred in Lancashire and sporting a walrus moustache, handled the message with amazement. 'Something's up,' was all he could think of to say. 'And something bad.' He seized his tall hat and trotted down the road to the inn where a sign read: 'Post Horses'. Within five minutes he was bound for Knowsley Hall, and in less than fifteen minutes he was at the massive doors of the front entrance.

He should not have been at the front entrance. But a nightmare vision of Thurloe pursuing him made him forget his station in life. It was a footman, answering his bell, who attempted to set him straight. 'Now, now, Mr Beech, you know better than this.'

Ordinarily Beech would have bowed to the inevitable. Now he swelled up a little. 'Most urgent telegraphic message here from the Prime Minister to Lord Stanley. Front door, rear door, it's all the same to me. If you don't want His Lordship to get it, I'll lump it.'

'Quite uncalled for, Mr Beech,' said the footman, surprised. 'I'm doing my duty, and well you know it. Let me have the message. I'll see what I can do.'

'*I'll see what I can do,*' repeated Beech. 'Not good enough,' and, with a quick step, he moved inside.

'Not quite so fast,' expostulated the footman, who was beginning to feel out of his depth. He looked behind him for support and was relieved to see the butler at the other end of the entrance-hall. He called out : 'Mr Morecombe !'

The butler made a sedate turn and bore down on them. Beech prepared for action : he twirled his moustache and folded his arms.

'Immediate delivery is utterly impossible,' ruled the butler, after hearing the story. 'His Lordship is engaged.' He did not condescend to explain the nature of the engagement. The truth was His Lordship was attending a rehearsal. Some members of the Oxford University Dramatic Society were at Knowsley Hall for a weekend. More, His Lordship was actually playing a part.

Mr Beech produced the message from an inner pocket and drew it out of the unsealed envelope. He held it almost under the butler's nose, and the butler found himself scanning it. He recognized instantly that it was in Latin because as a boy he had briefly attended a Jesuit school, and he caught the word Victoria. He also recognized other ominous Latin words. While he could by no means interpret it, he did get a general impression, and this sufficed to shake him to the marrow. A clock somewhere started to strike, which heightened the emotional impact, then other clocks throughout the vast rambling building took up the refrain, some with chimes.

Morecombe took the message with a feeling of foreboding, placed it on a silver salver, and marched to the doors of the rehearsal-room, which ordinarily was used as a ballroom. A stage was at one end.

What was in progress was a dress rehearsal of the famous scene from Shakespeare's *Richard III* set on the battlefield of Bosworth, where ancestors of the Stanley family played such an important part. Lord Stanley, in fifteenth-century costume, was taking the role of his illustrious predecessor. It was not in character for him to be doing this. He was shy, awkward, and fearful of meeting people, unlike his father, the rumbustious Earl, now on a sick-bed upstairs. But somehow he had been persuaded. The part was small; there was no audience. He was actually only filling in for someone else. The well-bred Oxford cast were all his guests. But somehow the climate changed with the entrance of Morecombe with a silver salver.

His Lordship at once evidenced irritation. 'Go away, Morecombe, go away.'

At this point, the young man who was directing the players called for a replaying of the concluding scene. Morecombe stood forlornly marooned in the centre of the ballroom. The noble Shakespearian lines began to roll, and then something odd happened. Morecombe marched forward and climbed the stage. Elocution halted, to be followed by a strained silence. The butler marched alongside Lord Stanley and whispered: 'My Lord, the Queen has been kidnapped!'

Lord Stanley stood like a statue. He knew his butler. Experience had taught him that when Morecombe said anything at all, which was rarely, it was precisely true. He took the message which was proffered him. It was a long one, yet, in a couple of minutes and despite the Latin, he was able to get to the heart of it, including the warnings and the *nuances*. The group of visiting Oxford actors meanwhile stood about in attitudes of elegant concern.

What ensued next happened rapidly. His Lordship lost all his diffidence. Summoning the butler to follow him, he made a beeline towards the steward's hall, where the the upper servants dined, which was some hundred and fifty yards distant, within the castle. He picked up Station-master Beech along the way. He delivered some instructions rapidly and asked some questions.

The upper servants, about twenty-five of them, were dining at that moment, and were being waited on by the lower orders, when His Lordship burst in on them. He rapped sharply on the table. They all began to rise, but he waved them down, and they resumed their places behind the soup-tureens, the bottles, and the massive candlesticks, startled as they had never been before. It had, for generations, been a point of honour – anyway, of protocol – for members of the Stanley family not to set foot in the steward's hall *while in use*, without permission, and the unwritten rule had persisted through the years. The rule was being rudely broken; in addition His Lordship was oddly dressed. Even the oldest retainers blenched.

Lord Stanley may or may not have guessed their thoughts. He spoke bluntly, staccato fashion: 'I have to tell you we are called to duty. Our Queen is in danger. Take this on trust from me at this time. I ask you ... Who here have been seamen?'

They took him on trust. Two men rose. The butler whispered: 'Briggs is the one, my Lord. The under-butler.'

'Briggs, your experience?'

'Shipbuilding at Laird's yards, my Lord; first mate on the paddle-steamer *Hyson*, with General Gordon in China.'

'Good! Be prepared to accompany me. Order a carriage. Have it at the door in less than five minutes. Quick, now!'

Briggs left on the run. A sort of sigh ran up and down the table.

'Soldiers here?' continued Lord Stanley.

Eleven rose. Three had seen service in the Crimea; three in the Indian Mutiny; one in Afghanistan; three in China; one even at Waterloo, but, as he was seventy-five years old and had to be helped from his chair, he was excused.

'Report to Morecombe. Off with your livery! Not a word of this to anyone...'

Twenty-five minutes later, Lord Stanley had performed the feat of getting out of Shakespearian costume, in a wildly rocking carriage, while bound for Liverpool. He was now walking along the windy dock area with Briggs. The waters of the River Mersey, about five furlongs wide at this point, were green and choppy.

They made their way to George's Dock, an incongruous couple, His Lordship tall and as thin as a rail, Briggs short and squat like a wrestler. As they turned a corner, past a public-house, the 'Mersey Arms', they had their first view of the *Phoebe*. She had two masts and two narrow yellow funnels, out of which came thin columns of smoke.

Briggs riveted his eye on her and muttered under his breath. 'She's fast. Built like the river-boat *Neptune*, only far bigger.

Paddle-wheels much bigger. Give her a head start and you'll never catch her.'

Three men were on her bridge. 'On guard and waiting all right,' continued Briggs out of the corner of his mouth, 'and steam up, too.' He led the way to the edge of the dock, where a two-foot-thick hemp fender kept the paddle-wheels from scraping the stonework. Seagulls swooped overhead. Something on the after-deck caught his attention. He stared fixedly and, judging by his quick breathing, he seemed to be excited. His gaze travelled to a huge crane which was stationed on the dock between the railway line and the water. Lord Stanley interrupted him:

'I have a feeling we are attracting attention, Briggs.'

The three men on the bridge were now watching them. About half a dozen other men, who had evidently been on the dock but not immediately visible, made an appearance in the distance. They seemed to be moving aimlessly, yet in their direction.

'Come along with me, Briggs,' said Lord Stanley. He began to move away. A steady course, with nothing hurried about it. But away. They were not followed.

'Did you see what I saw, my Lord?' enquired Briggs, still excited.

'I suspect not.'

'Did you observe the hold on the after-deck, my Lord?'

'I noticed there was a hold. Why?'

'My Lord, the hold on the *Phoebe* has been rebuilt. There isn't a ship I have seen that has that shape hold. More than twice as long as usual, maybe more.'

'What are you telling me, Briggs?'

'That hold is to receive something long, my Lord ... and unless I miss my guess that something is going to be dropped in by that crane.'

'Ha!' The exclamation was forced from Lord Stanley. It expressed volumes. He realized instantly that they had come upon a vital piece of information that must be relayed to the Prime Minister as fast as possible. The conspirators were not going to take a chance of being separated from their quarry at the waterfront. There wasn't going to be any separation. They, along with the Queen and the royal coach, were going to be dumped into the *Phoebe*.

'How many tons will that crane manage?' he asked.

'Fifteen tons maximum from my observation.'

Would the Queen's coach be within that maximum? Lord Stanley wondered. He assumed so. Only lunatics would concoct such a damnably elaborate plot without checking *that* item. He recalled having seen the coach about five years ago. He remembered it as being quite small, ten to twelve tons at a guess, if that. Plenty of leeway. They were back at the 'Mersey Arms', and round two more corners, well hidden, his coachman was waiting. Lord Stanley gave orders to Briggs: 'Wait here and watch. Move around. If you see trouble coming, evade it at all costs. No adventures. You'll have reinforcements within the hour. They'll be in disguise. Don't ask me what we can do with them because I don't know.'

'Board that damn' ship and seize it, my Lord,' said Briggs.

'Touch that ship, and they may kill the Queen.'

'I know it, my Lord. But I had to say something.'

Lord Stanley returned at the same wild speed to Knowsley, and there was met by the butler.

'Another message, my Lord.'

His Lordship took it hurriedly. Again it was in Latin, but this time it was short and uncomplicated:

'Urgent. LNWR officials inform me of possibility of Queen's train and Prince's train, which seems to be following closely, as well as my train, reaching Carstairs Junction at approximately same time. 9 p.m. is time mentioned. Our hope is some action can be agreed upon there. Meet me at Carstairs. Utmost caution required. My train travelling as Theatre Arts Society Special.'

There was no signature nor indication that this had emanated from Disraeli (none was needed), and there was no mention of Sir John Cowell's part in the undertaking. Carstairs Junction, as Lord Stanley well knew, was about fifteen miles distant, not far from Wigan, and within the boundaries of his own estates. It was a curious wilderness where railway lines came together, not in an ordered fashion, but more like wandering tendrils – an outcome of the speculative railway mania of the period. There were numerous platforms, and, near the middle of the complex, was an anachronism, a low, rambling, medieval coaching-inn, which had become divorced from the highway (which had been moved elsewhere) and now catered for the iron horse and its passengers. You could get a drink at the 'Carstairs Inn' at any hour of the day or night : long, long ago one of the innkeepers had done a Sovereign a service and had been amply rewarded.

'Who brought this message, Morecombe?'

'A station porter, my Lord. He is still here. Mr Beech, the station-master, returned to his post as, I believe, you instructed.'

'I did so instruct him. And I have an urgent message to send. Have the porter take it. Are your men out of livery and ready?'

'Yes, my Lord.'

'Good. We proceed to Carstairs Junction. Order two more carriages. Bring six men. Have six others – the best shots we have – report to Briggs, as invisibly as possible, at or near the "Mersey Arms". Their guns are to be concealed.'

Ten minutes passed.

Lord Stanley found himself pondering the final sentence of the Prime Minister's message : 'My train travelling as Theatre Arts Society Special.' By a coincidence, his own theatrical costume still lay in a heap on the carriage seat where he had discarded it.

Six retainers now came trotting out of a side-door. They were disguised all right. They could be taken for labourers, hucksters, buskers, sailors, or porters. Morecombe had even assumed the character of a travelling salesman, with a carpet bag and a tall hat. They climbed into two carriages.

Lord Stanley in his carriage gave the signal : they were off.

8

In certain seasons, a long period of twilight prevails in the north of England, and the scenery assumes soft colours. The Queen, imprisoned in her train, knew the country quite well and judged they were close to Preston. She bent down, fumbled in her reticule, and brought out a photograph. It was taken in March 1863, on the day of the wedding of Bertie, Prince of Wales, to the Danish princess, Alexandra. To say that it was an unusual wedding picture would be an understatement. The bridal couple were shown appropriately, to be sure, standing more than a little stiff and solemn. But it was she, the Queen, who occupied the central position. She was seated, dressed in deepest mourning, and *she* was gazing conspicuously, as well as sorrowfully, *away* from the bridal couple towards, and at, a marble bust of her Albert.

It was a Victorian picture with a story, indeed, many stories. There were those, maliciously inclined no doubt, who claimed that on this, the most important day of two young lives, the Queen was delivering a pictorial sermon that would be with them for ever ... 'In the midst of life we are in death.' 'How much more sublime was your father than you, Bertie.' 'Observe who holds the centre of the stage, Alex.' 'Let this be a lesson to you, Bertie.' 'Your dear father will always be here to haunt you.'

The Queen was aware of some of these interpretations. Only she knew the truth, which was quite simple. She was gazing fixedly at the bust of Albert because it was impossible for her to do otherwise, once she had made the decision that *he* should be in the family picture. She revealed her real feelings.

She wished to be with him.

She wished she were dead.

She had always been indifferent to real danger (minor alarms sometimes upset her), but now she was remorselessy indifferent – an aspect of her character that had not entered into the calculations of the conspirators.

She addressed herself to the Poet Laureate, who was resting with arms folded, a muscular, beared Buddha.

'Mr Tennyson.'

'Yes, ma'am?'

'How thick would you say is that compartment partition?'

'No more than a quarter or half an inch, ma'am.'

'That is what I thought. And they are sitting immediately behind that?'

'Yes, ma'am.'

'Can we identify their positions?'

'We can try, ma'am.' He regarded her curiously. What did she have in mind?

'And how would you do that, Mr Tennyson?'

The Poet Laureate shambled from his seat. The partition was at the rear end of the royal coach; in front of it was a low couch on which Mary Nolan was sitting, bolt upright, as did all those whose duties kept them close to the Queen. She moved aside nervously as the poet advanced. Marking a spot where he thought one of the men might be sitting, he put an ear against the wood. The outcome was unsatisfactory. He grunted. 'I can hear very faint noises, I believe, ma'am. Vague though. Can't identify them. The confounded engine is making too much noise.' He tried again. 'What we need is Dr Jenner's stethoscope. That would do the trick.'

'Capital idea,' agreed the Queen. 'If we can ever obtain it. I seem to remember that, when I was a child, we played a game of listening through inverted drinking-glasses.'

Tennyson looked at her and was puzzled. Diplomats and those who had a reason to value the spoken word praised the Queen's voice for its musical quality, a delicacy of intonation, almost unmatched in the kingdom. Now the voice had subtly changed. The music had become harsh. The tones were flatter. One could not go as far as say there was a trace of menace, yet there *was* a difference, and it was apparent to her two companions, although it might have escaped the notice of others. They knew something was in the wind: they both began to show concern.

'Might I ask, ma'am . . .' began Tennyson.

'Later, Mr Tennyson. Later. Kindly indulge my royal prerogative, even though I am helpless at the moment. Mary, please bring Mr Tennyson a glass tumbler. We shall experiment.'

Mary disappeared into the bedroom, little more than a cubicle, at the front end of the coach. When she returned her hand was shaking.

The poet took the tumbler, placed it against the wall with his ear to the bottom end, and moved it around a few times. 'Seems to be something here, ma'am. At this spot.'

'Mark it,' exclaimed the Queen. 'Mary, my bottle of ink. My pen.'

When Mary returned the Queen told her to give the ink and pen to Tennyson. 'Draw an outline, please,' she said.

The poet did his best, but it was hard labour for him.

'Now the other side.'

When it was over, two sketches defaced the partition. The lines were harsh and jagged. The effect was macabre.

The Queen appeared satisfied. Her eyes glinted. 'A beginning, Mr Tennyson. The next step will be more difficult ... Two pistols ... or preferably, two rifles ...'

If the Queen was about to say anything further, it was interrupted by a cry from Mary Nolan: 'No, ma'am, please!'

'Quiet, Mary. If you are thinking about yourself, I hope we can devise some way to get you out. If you are thinking about me, you are wasting your time.'

'They have taken precautions, ma'am,' urged Mary.

'They have!' exclaimed the Queen, speaking very slowly and weighing each word. 'What precautions? How do *you* know? Why do you say such a thing?'

Mary shook her head. 'It stands to reason, ma'am. I don't see how they could dare these frightful risks without taking everything into account. They've made provisions, depend on it ... Probably any shot from this direction will ignite the powder ...' Mary was becoming more and more agitated. Her voice was rising. She was wringing her hands.

A long pause followed. Tennyson seemed impressed, but, then, *his* world was always peopled with ladies in various stages of distress. The Queen, on the other hand, gave no outward sign of responding one way or the other. She was pursuing a chain of thought of her own. Finally she said: 'Sit down, Mary.'

Mary sat down.

The Queen turned to the poet.

'May I count on you, dear friend?'

'Indeed, ma'am ...'

'I thank you for your support from the bottom of my heart. I believe I know what you were about to say. You wish to warn me of the risks. I am indifferent to the risks.'

'Your obedient servant, ma'am.'

'Mr Tennyson, there is a small window in the lavatory attached to my bedroom. The engine is just ahead of us. Could you find a way to communicate with the engine-driver?'

'Let me investigate, ma'am.'

He stalked into the tiny room and pulled up the window. There was just enough space to get his head out. The engine, he found, was not attached directly to the coach, for, in between, was a small tender. His angle of vision wasn't good. Now and again he could catch a view of one shoulder of the driver, but how to attract his attention presented a problem that at the moment was beyond him.

He returned to the coach and was surprised to see the Queen standing in a corner absorbed in the contents of a small cabinet. He reported briefly, and she said, 'Mr Tennyson, this cabinet meant nothing to me when it was installed. I objected to it. I have never used it. I was given to understand it was some sort of system of electrical communication. I fear I have been mistaken.'

'In what way, ma'am?'

'Albert would have welcomed it. You recall how he delighted in innovations?'

'Those that served mankind, ma'am. Yes, he did. The Great Exposition was evidence enough.'

'Of course. Of course ... can this be of service to *us*?'

The poet prodded it gingerly with a finger. He was the least practical of men when mechanical or related matters were involved. He had no ideas about it at all. He observed two rows of switches in a setting of purple velvet. The switches were numbered one to ten. Alongside them were several small white squares about one inch across.

'There must be some key, some explanation,' said the Queen. Her chubby fingers began searching in the satin lining of the mahogany lid. She gave a muffled exclamation and produced a piece of paper that had evidently reposed in a pocket. What was written on the paper was cryptic enough:

'*Code of Signals*
(1) Signals All is Well.
(2) Emergency. Halt instantly.
(3) What is present speed of train?
(4) Reduce speed.
(5) Increase speed.
(6) Stop at next station.
(7) Stop now. Dressers are required.
(8) Stop now. Refreshments required.
(9) Stop now. Queen wishes to communicate with staff.
(10) [was blank].'

The Queen took it to the window and examined it closely. She passed it to Tennyson. 'Mr Tennyson, I have been not only wrong but foolish. An admirable system, I see now. Most practical. Is it working?'

'There is another question, ma'am,' put in the poet. 'Does this connect with the guard, the driver, or both?' They sat side by side, weighing the possibilities. Switch Number 3 was their initial choice. It simply called for information. It did not involve a commitment. The Queen herself manipulated it. They stared at the box as the seconds passed and attempted to envisage the astonishment of the recipient, whoever he might be. They were rewarded by a slight noise, a click. Two little shutters had slipped aside on two of the small squares disclosing the numerals 4 and 5 in that order.

'It works, ma'am! Forty-five miles an hour, evidently.'

'Yes ... too fast,' said the Queen, tonelessly. For the moment she had forgotten she no longer controlled destinies, hers or anyone's ... 'Try the window again, Mr Tennyson. Someone may be alerted.'

When the poet put his head out the second time, he found he had company. The guard was leaning out in the rear of the train. Up front, on the engine footplate, the driver was turned round and was looking back; he saw the poet, and gestured. He then began clambering on to the tender; when he had travelled as far as he was able, he was little more than an arm's length away. The driver was, of course, McCloskey, the veteran with the moleskin trousers.

'Stay there!' yelled Tennyson, using his massive voice to good effect, and retreating immediately into the coach. 'We are in communication, ma'am!'

The Queen nodded. 'Can we convey a written message?'

'It should be possible.'

She nodded again and began to write on the familiar paper with the heavy black margin, and headed, oddly enough in view of the circumstances: Windsor Castle.

'To my loyal subjects –

I call upon any of you to deliver two pistols, or two rifles, with ammunition, to Mr Tennyson.

Victoria R'

The poet bore back this message to the lavatory. In the meantime, the driver had got hold of a coaling-hook, used to poke into the recesses of the fire-box, and he was waving it on a level with the window – a handy instrument for impaling and conveying a message. Tennyson paused. The wind outside was heavy and it could easily rip a piece of paper off the hook. For safety, it should be tied. But with what? His hand moved tentatively to his cravat, then to his braces ... He took a couple of hesitant steps through a small side-door into the Queen's bedroom. A pile of clothes was heaped on a bed. On top of the pile was a pair of stays, conspicuously interlaced with laces. The poet was there with one step. He grasped a pair of scissors, which were lying on a bureau, and cut off a six-inch length.

He got no further with his plan.

He was shaken by a drumming, or pounding, noise, which seemed to be coming from somewhere inside the coach. The drumming stopped and was replaced by the more ominous noise of the gong. Tennyson leaped to the window and found himself staring at Todhunter who was leaning out of *his* window, and he had a pistol in his hand.

The alarmed driver scuttled to the middle of the tender, where he was out of sight and could get back to the footplate; the coaling-hook dropped to the tracks. In a moment, the train began braking to a stop.

Tennyson returned hurriedly to the Queen. He found her an accusing, blazing figure, staring at Mary Nolan.

'Our traitor – *there*, Mr Tennyson! I began to suspect it some time ago, but it seemed impossible. Why did they take from me the dresser who has been longest with me, and leave *her* here? ... She has betrayed us.'

'I heard a noise: a drumming,' put in Tennyson.

'Drumming, yes. She was warning them through the partition.'

A voice from outside called: 'Open the door!'

Mary Nolan opened it briskly, leaned down, and gave a hand to someone below on the tracks; and Todhunter appeared, head and shoulders first. He stood in the doorway blotting out the countryside, which, in this part of Lancashire, was made up of scattered farms and grey stone buildings.

The girl began whispering to him, as one accomplice to another. He nodded and kept glancing around the coach. First, at the outline sketches on the wall, next, at the cabinet with Mr Martin's electrical system, finally, at the piece of paper in the poet's hand. 'I'll take that,' he said. Tennyson handed it to him. The betrayal was thorough and complete.

Todhunter scanned the paper. 'You must think we are children.' he said with a grin. He walked to the cabinet, ripped aside the velvet and hammered what was underneath with his pistol-butt. He ripped away some wires. He studied the wall sketches. He turned to Tennyson.

'Out, Mr Tennyson! Out!'

The poet slowly let himself down to the ground.

Of those who had braved an early Scots morning at Ballater to accompany the Queen as passengers on the royal train with its three coaches, there remained only the guard, one valet, and Mary Nolan.

Others had been left by the wayside – Sergeant Collins, Lady Ely and Emile Dittweiler – or were aboard the Prince's train – Grey, Jenner, John Brown, and the police officers.

The ranks had thinned and were about to become thinner.

Todhunter leaned out of the door and signalled the guard who came up running.

'Unhook the last two coaches,' he ordered.

When the job was done he signalled to engine-driver Mc-Closkey. He spoke in a low voice, and only two words were audible: 'George's Dock'. McCloskey began to protest. He was cut short.

Three minutes perhaps elapsed before the train, or what was left of it, set off on the last leg of its journey. Tennyson, the valet and the guard, standing on the tracks by their marooned part of the train, watched the long front coach, containing the Queen of All the Britons, recede into the distance.

Some words came to the poet:

> ... But now the whole Round Table is dissolved
> Which was an image of the mighty world,
> And I, the last, go forth companionless,
> And the days darken around me, and the years ...

9

On board the Theatre Arts Special, nearing the disordered maze of railway lines known as Carstairs Junction, the Prime Minister felt that he now had as full a picture of the conspiracy and its intricacies as anyone in the kingdom – except those actually engaged in it.

The telegraph had been clattering all over the LNWR system and a stream of messages had been flowing to and from his train. One that gave him sombre satisfaction was from Manchester. It was an answer to one of his early enquiries, asking for the names of the three Fenians executed for the murder of the Manchester police officer, while they were attempting to free a fellow Irishman from a prison van. He showed it to Ponsonby without comment; then he asked the Colonel to accompany him to the second coach. Despite the pressures, he looked as debonair as ever. Ponsonby, as usual, looked like a rumpled professor.

In the second coach they found Lord Hastings asleep on his wife's shoulder, and Joe, the coachman, contemplating with satisfaction a half-emptied bottle, one of the perquisites of being a friendly witness. Mrs Larkin was sitting coldly upright.

'Mrs Larkin.'

There was no reply, and her face remained expressionless.

'Mrs Larkin, you *are* familiar with the names of Allen, Larkin, and O'Brien?'

'I am.'

'That is what I wish to confirm. You are, then, *the* Mrs Larkin?'

'I am the widow of the murdered John Larkin, if that's what you mean. He didn't fire the shot. He didn't kill the policeman.'

'We have been through all that, Mrs Larkin. You may profess not to understand the law, but I am abundantly certain that your husband understood it. He knew perfectly well that in such cases all participants suffer the penalty.'

He adopted the softer tone of voice that Queen Victoria found so irresistible. 'Tell me, would your husband countenance the awful conspiracy *you* are now engaged in? I cannot believe it.' If he was looking for a confession, he was disappointed.

Mrs Larkin held up her hand as though she was exorcising an evil spirit. 'No more, no more . . .' she said.

The Prime Minister eyed her intently, shook his head, and left, with Ponsonby following. As he returned to his seat, he realized that a heavy, rolling fog had begun to blot out the surroundings. At the same time, the train was slowing down almost to a walk.

He saw that Thurloe, the railway chief, had a door open and was peering at the ground.

'Carstairs,' shouted Thurloe.

Railway lights and signals were only barely visibly. A man waving a lantern shouted that the train was being switched to a line near the station-master's office. As they slowed to a bumpy halt alongside a low, tumbledown brick building, they passed close to the 'Carstairs Inn', from which the noise of singing was coming.

Lord Stanley came aboard immediately.

'The Queen's train?' Disraeli fired the question at him.

'About five miles away. We had been planning to delay it – if we could. Anything to gain time. The fog is providential.'

'A storm saved us from the Spanish Armada,' said Disraeli. 'Fog may help to save us now. How long will the train take to get here?'

'Fifteen to thirty minutes. More, if the fog persists.'

'When it gets here, can it be delayed further?'

'Our information is that it requires coal and water. Yes.'

'And the Queen's needs? Her welfare? How is she being treated now?'

'We do not know, sir . . . You are aware of the Tennyson affair?'

'I am. I understand that Tennyson was picked up by the Prince's train. So were the marooned coaches ... And where are the other trains?'

'Sir John Cowell arrived ten minutes ahead of you. Thanks to the fog, we were able to move the Prince's train around the Queen's train. It should be arriving now. The element of risk is great. These trains should not be moving.'

'Risks! Risks! Today there are no risks,' was the Prime Minister's comment. He continued : 'How are our forces distributed?'

'My men are in disguise here,' replied Lord Stanley. 'The railway has scores of others. Picked sharpshooters will be concealed, covering the Queen's coach. Their orders are to fire to kill only if both men can be caught outside their compartment at the same time. That isn't likely. Sir John Cowell has a squad of Highlanders with him. The situation at George's Dock is being watched closely by secret agents. Sharpshooters have been placed there. The Navy has three vessels standing by in the River Mersey. Every hundred yards of railway line from here to Liverpool is under guard.'

Lord Stanley led the Prime Minister along a black, foggy path to the station building. They came to a large working area where a group of men were clustered around a mass of charts and time-tables. 'Railway nerve centre,' he explained. 'They have managed to keep track of everything. Incredible job of organization. All traffic in this area has been brought to a standstill. The whole of the L N W R is on the alert. Damned disciplined structure, thank God . . .'

A door opened at the far end of the area and Sir John Cowell entered. Just behind him was the Duke of Marlborough.

In the meantime, a lonely figure was standing on one of the platforms debating what to do. The Reverend Charles Anderson had been told by Sir John Cowell to get off the Curates' Special train and that this was the end of the journey for him.

He had also been sworn to secrecy, although that wasn't necessary. He had gathered enough, by divination or otherwise, to grasp the scope of the whole horrific story. It oppressed him that he could take no part in it. Nor could he share his knowledge – which made him lonelier.

The fog was getting to be as bad as some of those he had known in his Limehouse parish, and he suspected worse was in the offing. He could hear a distant noise of a piano accompanied by singing. He made his way slowly in that direction. It was dangerous to cross the tracks: an approaching engine would be all but invisible; and his carpet bag was a hindrance. But he made it safely. He found he had come upon grimy whitewashed stone walls and a door with a sign over it, dimly illuminated by an oil-lamp: 'Carstairs Inn'.

He pushed the door open. Tobacco smoke was mingling with the fog which had crept inside, but at least there was plenty of light. It took him a few seconds to accustom his eyes to the scene. In front of him, and three steps down, there seemed to be a long series of rooms of differing sizes and shapes, as though someone had knocked together a whole row of ancient houses (which in fact was the case). At least three separate bars were operating, and gigantic casks, on stands, reaching as high as the ceiling, were labelled *Old Tom, Cream of the Valley, Out and Out,* etc. As he descended the steps and found himself a small table in a corner, which gave him a view of things, he saw that, owing to its straggling nature, the inn could accommodate all sorts of characters and still convey an illusion of separateness. At the far end, a group was carousing and dancing. A couple of buskers were doing an act accompanied by a piano – he had never seen a worse one. The crowd was mixed. The railwaymen were obvious, and there were plenty of them. There were tradesmen, commercial travellers, sailors, bargees, a few businessmen, a bevy of whores from Wigan, and there was one gentleman sitting near him who looked uncommonly stately and had a carpet bag just like his own. If *he* is a commercial traveller, mused the vicar, he sells either champagne or Bibles.

A serving-maid arrived and slapped his table with a cloth.

'What'll it be, Father?' she asked, and her Irish brogue was marked.

'Pint of porter, my dear,' he replied, matching her by slipping into an Irish accent. He thought: First curate, next vicar, and now promoted (or demoted) to Roman Catholic priest – that's a good one ...

The tensions of the day, which had kept him nervously alert until now, began to give way to weariness and he was nodding when the serving-maid returned with his porter. He drank and still remained bone-tired. His head drooped and he fell asleep where he sat.

There was also another lonely figure at the junction. This was the Duke of Cambridge. When the Prime Minister had left his train he had not seen fit to awaken the Duke from his slumber. Something eventually did awake him – probably the strange and unfamiliar noises from the inn. He began stirring, coughing, and cursing. His aide ran to his side.

'Where are we?' grunted the Duke.

'Carstairs Junction, sir.'

'Damme, there is no such place.'

Captain Adair was too well trained to contradict him. He said nothing.

'What are we doing here? Where's the Prime Minister?'

'The Prime Minister has gone off with Lord Stanley, sir.'

The Duke began heaving on his bunk. 'Why the devil wasn't I informed? I shall hold you to account for this, Adair.' He was off his bunk now. 'Take me to them immediately.'

The Duke was out of the room so fast that he either forgot or decided against buttoning on his sword. Compared with the Prime Minister, and those with him, whose everyday clothes merged into the enveloping fog, his Royal Highness was a semi-luminous and startling apparition. His tunic was red, his face was red, while his Field Marshal's cocked hat, with its white plumes, a rare sight even in London, and much more so in the provinces, fluttered bravely. Captain Adair, in a uniform derived from a Hungarian original, was following him, and was equally exotic. He was also completely at a loss which way to go, but decided not to reveal his ignorance. He turned left.

It was an unfortunate decision, not only because it was in the wrong direction, but because it led the two of them within the circle of light from an oil-lamp by the door of the 'Carstairs Inn' just as that door opened wide as customers and revellers were entering and leaving.

The martial spectacle, appearing from outer darkness, had an instant impact on the revellers, which was enhanced by the juxtaposition of the printed sign on the Prime Minister's train immediately in the rear: *Theatre Arts Society*. Nobody could be blamed for concluding that the two men were actors. They looked like actors, they walked like actors, and they were dressed like actors.

The prospect of entertainment, so close at hand, and seemingly heaven-sent, was too good to be lost, and, with cries of glee, some of the travellers embraced the couple and began jovially pulling them into the interior of the inn.

The Duke was taken completely by surprise. As the pulling

turned to shoving and hauling, he discovered he was so hemmed in that he had no leverage at all. He and the Captain were propelled forward and down the three inside steps.

'Draw your sword, Adair. Cut a way out of this,' hissed the Duke, uncontrollably furious.

The Captain needed no prompting. However, to draw his sword he needed a free arm. A large bearded sailor was forestalling him by holding his scabbard upside down. The Captain's efforts to overcome his handicap were frantic. Customers deserted bars and tables and watched in amused fascination. There were cries of 'Go it, little 'un.' Someone started a song, which was taken up by the pianist. Meanwhile, the Duke, breathing heavily, had been pressed into a chair. Drinks were offered to him, but he swept them on to the floor.

Throughout this episode, two customers remained unmoved. The Reverend Charles Anderson was in so deep a sleep that not even the entry of the Duke had awakened him; when the noises grew louder, mingled with music, singing, and shouting, he kept assuring himself that it was just one more of the brawls with which, in his Limehouse parish, he was only too familiar. It was only when he caught a sleepy glimpse of the Duke's red tunic through the wall of spectators that he became curious.

The commercial travaller, sitting near the vicar, also remained aloof, although *he* was very much awake and alert. His back was to the front door, and while he was aware that a devil of a rumpus was going on, he didn't have a full view of it. What was important – for him – was that he was under orders to stay in disguise. He was Morecombe, the butler.

The Reverend Mr Anderson forced himself reluctantly into motion. He rose from his chair. He stood on it. He saw an enraged, red-faced character who seemed vaguely familiar. He blinked as he struggled to recall the face, and the realization came to him like a thunderclap. He had seen the Duke only a couple of times at ceremonies at Westminster Abbey and St Paul's, and then from some distance. Even so, there was no doubt of it. This was the Duke.

He got down from his chair and turned to the commercial

traveller (that is to say, Morecombe). 'Incredible. That's the Duke of Cambridge they have there.'

Morecombe stood on *his* chair. He knew the Duke by sight, too, because he had seen him at the Earl of Derby's town house in London. He recognized him instantly. He stepped down, badly shaken. He paused for a moment, then raised his right arm and signalled to one of his invisible retinue (a busker). 'Get Lord Stanley here quickly,' he ordered. 'Find him.' He whispered the rest in his ear.

To the vicar he rasped: 'Please come with me, sir. Anything you can do to help, sir.' He began making his way to the rear of the inn, through rambling rooms, skirting casks and fireplaces, with the vicar close behind him. The two men found the inn-keeper behind a bar, a small man, with his hair plastered down and parted in the middle.

Morecombe, confronting him, pointed an ominous finger in the direction of the disturbance. '*That is the Royal Duke of Cambridge!*'

The Reverend Mr Anderson nodded confirmation. He added for good measure, 'Field Marshal. The one with the sword is his aide.'

The inkeeper's ferret-like eyes shifted warily. 'God's truth, Reverend?'

'I can't speak for God's truth,' replied the vicar, in his usual vein. 'I can only speak *my* truth, and that's the Duke all right. Offhand I'd say you'd be wise to clear up the situation in the next ten seconds.'

The innkeeper grasped a bung-starter and struck a ship's bell above the bar twice. This sound brought half a dozen men in leather and cloth aprons running from various doors. They all carried bung-starters. They swept through the circle of customers making merry at the expense of the Duke, and the innkeeper, in the lead, felled the large sailor with one well-aimed blow.

At that moment Lord Stanley arrived. The sight of His Lordship in the doorway produced a silence. Lord Stanley was not only a feudal lord with great powers, he was also the landlord of the countryside for miles around, and seven-eighths of the customers were his tenants.

He made no attempt to find out what was going on.

He said softly to the Duke, so that no one could overhear:
'The Queen has come.'

10

The Queen had indeed come, but she still remained alone. The
Prime Minister and the Prince of Wales stood side by side contemplating the solitary royal coach wreathed in fog, on a siding
at Carstairs Junction, a terribly moving yet unreal spectacle.

It has the quality of a nightmare, the Prime Minister mused.
Todhunter is nightmarish. So is the gong. This junction in the fog
is like Hades viewed across the Styx. The tangle of railway lines,
the sounds from the inn, not to mention other sounds, the diver-
sity of the characters involved, the impossibility of dealing ration-
ally with the situation – all these are a part of a dream state.
Perhaps I shall wake up.

The two of them walked wearily to the station offices. The
Prime Minister began talking in a low voice: 'Rescue, I know, is
the paramount question, sir. We will come to that. What I have
to say now, urgently, is that although these devils have the Queen
in their power, *they* are also in *our* power. Let us not forget that.
They hold the person of the Queen, yes, but they have to continue
to hold it. They have to get her to Ireland, where we assume they
hope to use her as a hostage. To gain this end, they must preserve
her life. They have to be careful, cautious. So I say, sir, we have
bargaining powers too.'

'We can bargain with madmen?'

The Prime Minister paused. 'I grant you that one of them –
Todhunter – may very well be mad. The other, McClune, is far
from mad. With your permission I propose to confront them.
Personally.'

'Good God. But the risk ...'

'What risk there is, is calculated. I am a calculating person, if
I may make a confession.'

The Prince considered this. He asked. 'What will you say to them?'

'I will say that the train doesn't move an inch unless I can talk to your mother. And after I talk to your mother, it still won't move an inch unless I am assured she is being well taken care of.'

'You would give them that ultimatum?'

'I would.'

'My mother would be placed in terrible jeopardy.'

'No more than at present ... There is another consideration, sir. Time is running against us. Liverpool and the ship are not far from Carstairs Junction. We need time. Any amount of time we can get.'

'What is the situation now?' asked the Prince.

'Their engine needs coal. Coal is being delayed on a pretext ... fog. For the moment they can't move.'

The Prince was resolving some inner conflict. At length he said, 'I must insist on accompanying you when you visit them, Mr Disraeli.'

The Prime Minister looked gratified. But he waved away the request. 'That *would* be dangerous, sir. You are the heir to the throne. At all costs, you must be kept out of this. To expose you would be to play into their hands.'

A few minutes later he was on his way to the Queen. He was alone. At first he had leaned towards taking either Ponsonby or Hartington with him; the first because he was reliable, the second because he was the heir to a dukedom. He had decided against both. He had tried to visualize the scene from the conspirators' point of view. He feared that the appearance out of the fog of two men might hint at a plot or a ruse. He preferred to gamble on the appearance of one man. He moved very slowly along the tracks under the protection of the hidden sharpshooters, although he was well aware that that protection was probably illusory. He came abreast of the single coach. Todhunter emerged out of the darkness; he had been prowling around.

'Who are you?' he rasped. He peered forward intently and began to answer his own question ... 'You! You!' He peered again as though he suspected a masquerade. 'It *is* you?'

'The Prime Minister,' said Disraeli.

'Are you alone?' demanded Todhunter. 'This must be a trick. There must be others.'

'There are no others. I am entirely alone.'

Captain McClune put his head out of his compartment window. His white face was barely visible. 'Have the Prime Minister stand at the foot of this door . . . Now, sir?'

'I wish to see Her Majesty,' said Disraeli, bluntly. He had considered making a last appeal on her behalf, but decided it was useless.

'Impossible,' interjected Todhunter. 'We allowed the Queen one visitor. Tennyson. You know how that was repaid.'

McClune interrupted. 'Quiet!' he said to Todhunter. 'I assure you the Queen is well. She will continue to remain well just as long as we are not interfered with. The non-delivery of coal is interference. Have it delivered instantly.'

'Coal will be delivered and this coach permitted to move on my order only,' replied Disraeli.

'Give the order then.'

'There will be no such order.'

'You understand that will be signing the Queen's death warrant?'

'I understand that. The Queen's, yours, mine, no doubt. Also the death warrant of all the Irish people, and all the hopes of Ireland. You choose *that* in preference to letting me have a brief audience with her? I find it hard to credit. I *am* Her Majesty's principal minister.'

There was a lengthy pause. McClune said reluctantly, 'You may go in. You will come out when you hear *this*.' He rapped once on the gong.

Disraeli bowed slightly and climbed up into the dim interior of the coach. An oil-lamp was burning low. Mary Nolan was sitting with her head against the partition. The Queen was by a small table which had a single lighted candlestick. She looked infinitely sad, and Disraeli felt his heart pounding. He dropped to his knee.

'Your Majesty.'

'Dear Mr Disraeli. We have met under happier circumstances.'

'You must not despair, ma'am.'

'I am very close to despair. My friends have been taken away. Mr Tennyson, is he safe?'

'He is quite safe. He was picked up by the Prince's train.'

'And my son?'

'Safe and well.'

'Where is he now?'

'It might be better not to divulge that, ma'am, if you will forgive me.'

'I understand. And John Brown, is he well?'

'Your faithful John Brown is safe. But terribly distressed.' Disraeli did not feel it expedient to mention that, as a result of the distress, Brown had been dead drunk for hours.

'How did all this happen, Mr Disraeli?' continued the Queen. 'Can you explain to me how gunpowder could be introduced into my own coach...?'

'We have a theory, ma'am. There are some grounds for it. Full verification will have to wait awhile. We believe it was slipped aboard at Ballinluig when one of the conspirators was engaging General Grey in conversation.'

'I was watching him from this very chair.'

'No doubt you were, ma'am. It was part of the plot to have all eyes focused on him as he stood on the platform. After all, he had succeeded in stopping a royal train. No one does that lightly. We suspect that while he was performing his part the other conspirator, with the help of accomplices, not known so far, was transferring cases of gunpowder into the other, or blind, side of the compartment. The cases were on trays to facilitate handling. It is probable that the whole undertaking took less than sixty seconds. Actually at the end of it they had time to spare.'

The Queen shuddered. 'Monstrous!'

'Monstrous, it is ... Dear lady, are you being cared for?'

'Those are very odd words, Mr Disraeli, to a Sovereign who has been abandoned and is a prisoner.'

'I don't know how else to put it, ma'am ... I quote Tennyson's poem: "I would that my tongue could utter the thoughts that arise in me". If I did start to utter them I would break down. I

139

must keep the questions simple, and enquire about humble matters. Is there anything you wish? Food?'

The Queen shook her head. Mary Nolan had offered her a sandwich and she had rejected it in horror. She persuaded herself it must be poisoned. She had no appetite since.

'Physical arrangements, ma'am?' continued Disraeli. He stared at Mary Nolan, and directed the rest of the sentence to her. 'Is everything taken care of?'

'The lavatory is out of water,' added the Queen dully. 'You speak of physical matters. Now I shall speak of spiritual matters. I have one wish, even if it is my last. I wish to take communion.'

Disraeli winced inwardly. It was an understandable request. None could foresee the end of the Queen's journey. But communion entailed a clergyman of the Church of England. Where could one be found?

The sound of a gong – not loud – made him look at his watch. He smiled reassuringly, which he could always do in any circumstances and in any company. 'I shall see what can be done, ma'am. Now I must say goodbye. The clock moves against us.'

He kissed her hand reverently and let himself down to the track.

McClune was peering at him.

'I have ascertained Her Majesty's last wishes,' said Disraeli, looking up. 'Water for the lavatory, and a clergyman to give communion.'

'Fifteen minutes,' was McClune's answer. 'Before you do anything else, deliver coal. That is *my* ultimatum.'

It was only a question of time before the Reverend Mr Anderson would be traced and summoned, and that time could be measured almost in seconds. He had just ventured upon a second glass of porter when he felt a tap on his shoulder and discovered that the station-master was standing behind him. 'If you would be so good as to come quickly to the office, Reverend. Quickly!'

'Who wishes to speak to me?'

'I am not at liberty to say, sir. Most urgent.'

The vicar swallowed what remained of his beer and clutched

his carpet bag, which contained two worn shirts, a nightgown, some sermons, a Bible, some correspondence from his bishop, and a prayer-book. He followed the lead of the station-master through the fog, which was just beginning to show signs of lifting. The breeze from the direction of the Irish Sea and the River Mersey was fresher. He was escorted into a room where, without warning, he found himself face to face with the Pomp of England – the Prince of Wales, the Prime Minister, cabinet ministers ... most of them seated round a table, but some standing. He wiped his mouth with the back of his hand to remove any trace of beer suds and placed his bag on the floor. It could not be said that he made any effort to travel under false pretences. The long day's ride had rumpled his clothes. He was what he was.

The Duke of Marlborough eyed him bleakly: 'This man is quite unfit to give communion to Her Majesty.'

'He is?' exclaimed the Prince. 'Why?'

'He doesn't even believe in prayer.'

Disraeli raised an eyebrow. 'Is that so, Mr Anderson?' He personally did not care in the least what the clergyman believed or didn't believe, so long as he was authentic.

'No,' answered the vicar. 'I believe in prayer, but at the proper time. I had a discussion with His Grace in the train. We disagreed. He wished me to pray for the Queen. I took the view that what we needed and what the Queen needed was *action* on earth.'

Disraeli instantly decided this was his man. At the same time he was cautious.

'You *are* in Holy Orders, sir?'

'Oh yes.'

'You can administer Holy Communion?'

'Yes.'

'To the Queen?'

'Yes.'

'Do you *believe* in Holy Communion?' asked the Duke of Marlborough sullenly.

The Reverend Mr Anderson ignored the question.

'Your parish?' continued Disraeli.

'Limehouse.'

'You have verification, no doubt?'

The vicar pointed to his carpet bag. 'There.'

Some whispered words passed between the Prime Minister and the Prince, then Disraeli said, 'I have no idea why fate brings this particular member of the cloth here at this time. We happen to be in need of one; there are no others available ... Who *are* you, Mr Anderson? What do you believe in? Are you a Fenian agent? Don't answer these questions. It doesn't matter. There isn't time to check on any of it. We must take things on trust ... You are going to be with the Queen for the last few miles in England. What will happen, God knows. Our aim is to rescue the Queen – if we can. You will be in the position of emissary. You will use your eyes and ears and you will appear guileless, and one other thing: you will find out what you can about the Nolan woman ... Hartington, proceed, will you?'

Hartington rose from his chair, and a spectator attempting to describe the movement might settle on the word 'languorously'. The heir to the dukedom of Devonshire remained unhurried as always. Behind the façade, however, was an intelligence that was capable of going to the heart of things, although, in the society in which he mingled, it was wise of him to keep this concealed. While on the Prince's train, Hartington had listened for several hours to proposals to rescue the Queen and had studied others that had been telegraphed from the Prime Minister's train. A few were ingenious.

Dr Jenner had advanced the idea of chloroform. It would be piped into the conspirators' compartment through the oil-lamp aperture in the roof. The vision of the conspirators collapsing in the midst of their gunpowder, caught without a struggle at the centre of their spider's web, seemed too good to contemplate. The plan seemed to solve everything – until it was realized that the windows of the compartment, both of them, remained open at all times. The chloroform would soon be dissipated.

As befits a soldier, General Grey had presented a simple and straightforward plan: he recommended shooting the two men through the partition – the plan in fact that had been put forward by the Queen herself, although at the time Grey had no means of knowing that. The idea died when the marooned Tennyson was picked up, and it was learned that such an attempt had been under way and had been discovered.

A more violent form of attack – pouring a fusilade of shots into the compartment from a train running alongside – was vetoed by the Prince as being too dangerous. He made the point that it only required the reflex action of one finger for the conspirators to fire the gunpowder: a dying reflex would be just as effective as a living one. Besides, the fusilade might make a direct hit on the powder.

A variation – to halt the Queen's coach somewhere, or wait until it was halted at George's Dock, and then pour in a concentrated fire from sharpshooters – was also vetoed by the Prince at first. Later it was held in suspense. 'It might have to come to that,' the Prince said, 'but only I will make the decision, and I will make it only at the instant involved or just before.'

There were other plans: getting sharpshooters on to the roof and shooting down; getting them underneath and shooting up; using a high-pressure stream of water . . .

Hartington was aware of all this background when he was called on by the Prime Minister. There was simply not time to review it.

'Proposals for rescue so far,' he said, 'fail to take one danger into account. A dangerous omission. The Nolan woman is alongside and in control of the Queen. She is presumably armed. If the conspirators are killed and she is not killed, what happens to the Queen? We have no reason to assume that, having gone thus far, Nolan will have a change of heart at the last moment. She is in the company of assassins; she is one of them; she will act like one. The first step must be to seize Nolan . . .' He turned to a diagram on the wall, a large-scale drawing of the Queen's coach done hurriedly by the railway staff. 'How can this be done? Smuggle someone into the coach – in addition to this clergyman. I draw your attention to the sketch of the lavatory window. Mr Tennyson, who has had experience with it, estimates that the lower part lifts nine or ten inches. He could put his head out, but not much room was left. There is probably enough room to get someone through . . .'

'Who?' put in the Prince, beginning to get excited again. 'Who is small enough? And they are watching both sides of the train. What makes you think *this* will succeed, Hartington?'

'We have an example of success, sir. They smuggled in the gunpowder at Ballinluig. They did it by creating a diversion.'

'Well?'

'We can create a diversion.'

'Where?... Here?... How?'

'No, further down the line would be safer. A brass band, an apparent railway wreck, anything that will draw them to one side of the train for sixty seconds, yet won't alarm them too much – that's what I mean by diversion: an excuse for the engineer to slow down without rousing suspicion.'

'Then what?'

'We get someone through the window. That person stays hidden in the lavatory, or in the bedroom. At the right moment that person is available.'

'What is the right moment? Available for what?'

'I can't answer that,' responded Hartington. 'No one can. The moment may not come. I am unable to see into the future. All we can hope for is that someone will be there when opportunity offers. Someone with weapons. Jenner's chloroform is a possibility. It is silent and effective ... Mr Anderson will have to make the decisions.'

'I don't like it,' said the Prince. 'God knows this is not the place for a stranger. Can't someone here *act* as a clergyman? Knollys? Cowell? Ponsonby?'

Disraeli gestured dissent. 'McClune knows everyone here by sight. Impossible.'

'Then it is up to you, Mr Anderson,' continued the Prince. 'God save her, you, and us. What do you say?'

'All I can say, sir, is: God willing, I am ready. How do we maintain communications? The diversion – how am I to be kept informed?'

'You'll know when there's a diversion because the train will stop,' said Hartington. 'It will take a minute or two to get some-

144

one through the window. If we run into trouble, it may take longer.'

'And then?'

'Keep quiet, and keep the Queen quiet. Communications will have to be improvised. Let us say a signal for action will be a red flag. Someone waving a red flag. At that signal, silence Nolan. Be careful about it. *Silence* her, don't kill her.'

A clock struck the quarter-hour with a noise not unlike a gong, a reminder that caused expressions of concern to flit across a score of faces and, for a few seconds at least, the company was frozen into immobility. Outside the fog-bound window a red signal light flickered. The Reverend Mr Anderson appeared a rather pathetic figure, surrounded as he was by peers of the realm, most of whom, as he knew, held it against him that he should have turned up at all. He could interpret their train of thought without trouble: The Queen deserves a better fate; she deserves a clergyman who is a gentleman. He blew his nose on a large blue handkerchief.

The Prime Minister broke the spell. 'You must go immediately. Station-master, you escort him. We'll not advertise the importance of this visit. Leave your carpet bag here, Vicar. Take only what you need.'

Soon after that, the Reverend Mr Anderson was stumbling along the track. Todhunter was waiting for him when he reached the coach. 'Once bitten, twice shy,' he said. 'You will be searched.'

The vicar submitted. The search uncovered an ancient, miniature penknife (a present from a parishioner), which he was allowed to retain, and (fortuitously) the most recent letter from his bishop (another reproof on the subject of his unorthodox views), which set at rest all suspicions of his authenticity. He was getting ready to climb into the coach when he heard the bad tidings. 'Let me warn you,' said Todhunter, 'that all blinds will be drawn from this point onward. Don't try to communicate; don't try sending messages or receiving them. Don't try any tricks. It will be fatal.'

The Queen viewed with resignation the shabby, almost un-

145

kempt, clerical figure who clambered into her coach, shoving odd articles on to the floor ahead of him. There was an old Bible and a prayer-book, an old medicine bottle, apparently filled with wine, and a piece of bread wrapped in an old newspaper.

'The Reverend Charles Anderson, ma'am,' said the vicar, who had trouble at first adjusting himself to the subdued light, or rather lack of it. He took out his handkerchief and wiped his glasses. Out of the corner of his eye, he saw Mary Nolan on the divan, and she surprised him. He had conjured up a picture of a hard-faced woman with a thin mouth. He found a girl with large blue eyes. 'Of such material are martyrs made,' was the thought that instantly came to him. He was chilled at the revelation. As for the Queen, he was not prepared for anyone so diminutive, barely five feet tall, he estimated. The face was chalk-white, a pallor which was accentuated by the contrast with the coal-black dress.

She spoke almost tonelessly, 'Is your parish here, Mr Anderson?'

'No, ma'am, I happen to have been attending a church conference in Scotland. I am on my way home and was in the station.'

'Scotland,' repeated the Queen, as if it were a place that she had loved and lost long, long ago, and would never see again. 'Do you happen to know the Reverend Norman Macleod? So warm, so compelling. I place him first among the churchmen I have known.'

'I regret to say I'm not acquainted with him, ma'am. If I may say so, we need more warmth in our pulpits.'

'You are quite right,' said the Queen. 'I have always thought so.' A tiny, and unanticipated, flame of interest had been kindled. The Queen had always been intensely interested in church and scriptural matters. Perhaps this clergyman was not what he seemed to be.

'If I may use your table, ma'am,' said the vicar. 'I thank you ...' The Queen removed her diary, her Bible and a reticule from the small table beside her chair, and the vicar deposited on it his medicine-bottle and the bread. 'A humble service indeed, ma'am. Not fit for a Queen. In my parish at Limehouse we do better than this, and there is probably none poorer. I should like a white tablecloth of some kind ... and I should like to wash my hands.'

The Queen motioned in the direction of her bedroom and the lavatory. 'There was no water there an hour ago.'

'Water is there now, ma'am,' said Mary Nolan.

The vicar walked to the lavatory and closed the door. The window was shut and he cautiously prised it open. He examined the catch and found it to be an elementary swivel. He pulled out his tiny penknife, and had no difficulty with the two small screws that held it in place. The catch came away in his hands; he hurled it into the fog. Further examination showed that the window opening could be no more than nine inches. Getting anyone in would be a hazardous business. How could a grown man manage it? He washed his hands, dried them on his handkerchief, and took down a small white towel that appeared to be unused. A label in one corner read: LNWR. As he emerged he wondered whether, in all the history of the railway, one of its towels had ever been used as an altar-cloth.

He began thumbing through *The Book of Common Prayer*. 'If your Majesty pleases, the shorter service of "Communion of the Sick" would seem the most appropriate.'

'I am not aware that I am sick, Mr Anderson.'

'The word in this case has a broad interpretation, ma'am. The service has the virtue of being brief and simple, and we do not have much time. The service is primarily intended for those whose infirmities prevent them from attending church. But others besides the physically sick are unable to attend: soldiers on the battlefield, and persons incarcerated in prison. I would say, ma'am, that you are in the latter category.' He handed the prayer-book to the Queen. 'If your Majesty cares to make use of it – I know it by heart.' He smoothed out the towel and broke the bread in pieces, returning a large piece to the newspaper for possible separate use later. He had the feeling that the Queen was hungry. He looked around for glasses for the wine, and spied a pair of them on a silver tray by a carafe. As he set them down, the coach gave a jerk, then began moving gently and without warning. There was no whistle from the engine nor sign from the junction. From the other side of the partition, three sharp raps sounded. Mary

Nolan at once responded from her side with three raps. The meaning seemed clear: 'All's well.'

The service was over, and the Queen sat with bowed head. The silence was eventually broken by the vicar, who was anxious to prevent the Queen from brooding too much, and, although it was in violation of protocol to initiate a conversation in her presence – one of the court customs he had read about – he decided to do it anyway. He was not reproved.

'Ma'am, do you know what led *her* to do this thing?' He kept his eye away from Mary Nolan, but it made little difference. If she heard, she gave no indication.

'I do not, and I do not care to discuss it. She was placed as a spy in my household. Who would have thought it? Who would have suspected it?'

It was on the tip of the vicar's tongue to say: 'It is the face that puzzles me; I do not detect wickedness in the ordinary sense.' But he refrained. The Queen knew only one sort of wickedness and one sort of goodness, and there were no grey areas in between. Instead, he began another question, but he got no further than the word 'motive' before he was cut short. 'The motive doesn't interest me, Mr Anderson. Betrayal is enough.'

I shall have to feel my way carefully, thought the vicar. Yet the Prime Minister had requested information. After a pause he ventured, 'If I do not presume too much, ma'am, may I put a question to *her* directly?'

The Queen was obviously displeased. She never made any attempt to conceal her feelings, and she did not now. Several seconds elapsed before she answered: 'We are totally indifferent.'

The vicar turned to the girl: 'I am using my prerogative as a minister. I am not attempting to cross-examine you. What *was* your motive?'

'My country and people,' said Mary Nolan.

'But what has *this* crime got to do with patriotism? This is madness. Surely.'

'Yes, it is madness.'

'You have thought of the effect on your family? This will utterly destroy them.'

148

'My family is already destroyed ... most starved, some were executed, some were deported, some died while emigrating ...'

'You are alone then?'

'Yes.'

'Have you no qualms?'

'I have many. When the hangman's noose is in front of me, I shall sing *God Save the Queen* and mean every word of it.'

The Queen acknowledged this remark with a look of concentrated venom. The vicar momentarily forgot that he had to be cautious. 'I do not understand you. You admit that this is madness, but you don't appear mad to me.'

'Dying for a cause is a form of madness, isn't it?' said Mary Nolan. 'Personally, we have nothing against Her Majesty. Nothing. Some drastic deed was necessary to focus attention on English abominations in Ireland.'

'You have been long in this plot?'

'From the beginning.'

'And you were able to hoodwink everyone?'

'Yes. The hardest part was appearing innocent.'

'You appear flippant. Is that what you really intend?'

'Since you ask me, no. It's a pose.'

'I am sorry for you.'

'Thank you, but it's too late.'

Unexpectedly, the train began drawing to a halt. The brakes were being applied quickly. Outside, there were noises, growing louder, that suggested crackling and burning. The vicar instinctively pulled aside a corner of the drawn blinds, but a sharp word from Mary Nolan made him move away. She slid to one end of the divan, and held her blind open a few inches. Some sort of railway van had overturned and was in flames. Railwaymen with hoses were blocking both lines. Two sharp raps came from the other side of the partition; Nolan responded with two raps ... Warning signal given; warning signal acknowledged, was how the vicar read it. His rate of breathing increased because he knew what was coming. This was the rendezvous. He tried to make it appear that he was immersed in the prayer-book. He listened for the hint of a noise from the lavatory and kept his eyes away from there, but the racket arising from the wreck and flames drowned all other noises. Mary Nolan's fingers drummed on the woodwork. What she said was barely decipherable: 'Done deliberately.' The vicar raised his eyes from the book and kept them expressionless, he hoped. He found himself reciting, half audibly, that most powerful passage: 'We brought nothing into this world, and it is certain we can carry nothing out. The Lord gave, and the Lord hath taken away ...'

Five minutes must have elapsed before the sounds outside started to die down. It became possible to hear voices. There was a cross-current of orders and shouting. The rasping voice of Todhunter was distinguishable. The voices stopped. The coach began moving backwards and continued for perhaps fifty yards when it halted, and forward progress began again, obviously on another track.

What next? speculated the vicar. Fate has put me into the front pages of history. Me, of all people, and I am not equipped to handle the task – but for that matter no one else seems to be equipped either. The effect that total surprise can have on a society such as ours is staggering. There is a lesson here that bodes ill for the future ... Further speculation was interrupted when Mary Nolan gave a rap on the partition and followed it up by four separate raps. A single-rap response followed. Whatever the message, it had been understood and acknowledged. Communication was being maintained. She rose with the words: 'Keep your places,' and walked quickly through the open bedroom door into the lavatory. The vicar stiffened in alarm. The moment he had anticipated with dread – at some time in the future – was the instant moment and there had been no time for preparation. He heard what seemed to be a stifled cough followed by a sharp thud, a groan.

The vicar was at the lavatory door in one bound. He pulled it open and his arms were suddenly full of Mary Nolan who was slumping backwards. He stumbled a couple of steps and let her drop clumsily to the floor. A knife was sticking in her heart. In the lavatory, crouching, was a young woman dressed in black – Skittles Walters.

'What have you done?' demanded the anguished vicar.

'She took me by surprise,' replied Skittles. 'I daren't let her give the alarm. I had to do it.'

The vicar was kneeling on the floor. He was no physician, but it was clear that the wound was fatal. Blood was spurting copiously.

'Who are you?' demanded the Queen. 'Who sent you?'

'Catherine Walters, ma'am. The Prince sent me.'

'My son sent you! I don't believe it. How dare you!'

'She is dead,' interjected the vicar. 'God only knows what will happen now.' He fumbled to reach the prayer-book, riffled through the pages, and began reciting a prayer.

'The Prince did indeed send me,' continued Skittles. 'So did Lord Hartington and Mr Disraeli ...'

An expression of abhorrence came over the Queen's face. She suddenly grasped whom she was dealing with. Tennyson had first mentioned the name, and at that time she had suspected the worst.

The girl before her was slim, pretty, hard as nails. 'They found no one else could climb in through the window except me, ma'am,' continued Skittles. 'They hadn't planned it that way, although I think Lord Hartington had it in mind. He told me to stand ready.'

A tear trickled down the Queen's cheek. 'To what am I reduced!' she murmured.

The vicar concluded his prayer. He rose. Drained as he had been by a cross-current of emotions, he seemed to have become a different man. A plan had formed in his mind and he intended to carry it out in sequence. There was at least a chance it would take care of some of the dangers to come. To the distraught Queen he said: 'Ma'am, if you will take your seat. Thank you.' The Queen did.

The next step was momentous. He inferred that the last signal given by Mary Nolan was a warning that she was going to be away from her post – and perhaps the four raps signified an estimated absence of four minutes, but this was speculation. What was certain was that in one way or another she would report her return. Would she report with the three-rap signal which he diagnosed previously as being an 'all clear' sign? Or with some other signal? He decided to risk three. He took a deep breath and tried to imitate her pattern of rapping, same weight, same speed. The pause of a few seconds that followed made him feel years older. But an answering three raps came.

He left the divan and said to Skittles: 'We've got to get this body out through the window. Help me.' He had decided that to keep it could prove fatal – to the Queen, if not to all of them. To get rid of it would entail a terrifying risk, yet with a possibility of reprieve. He had already concocted the story he would tell, if it came to that.

He took the dead girl's shoulders while Skittles took the feet. He closed the bedroom door out of deference to the Queen. He pulled out the knife. Truly a martyr, was the thought that came to him. She would be enshrined in Irish hearts for ever. Aloud he said: 'Feet first!'

He took the brunt of the weight and the two of them got the feet through the window. The train took a sharp curve, and for a moment they were unbalanced, staggering under the burden. On the outside there was a spectacle – a nightmare – of a solitary coach moving through the night in the direction of Liverpool, with one half of a woman protruding over the track.

'Now the rest,' puffed the vicar. It was a squeeze, but they managed it. There was a blast of air. Mary Nolan vanished. The vicar hurled the knife after her and found himself repeating familiar words: 'I am the resurrection and the life, saith the Lord ...' Skittles did not appear to be listening. She grabbed a towel and a pillow-case, muttering, 'Blood everywhere! Get rid of it! Get rid of it!' and got down on her knees doing just that. It was while she was in the midst of this that she looked up and suddenly announced: 'I have a message.'

'What message?'

She pulled out a bloodstained piece of paper. The vicar opened the bedroom door to take advantage of the larger oil-lamp. The message read:

'Do absolutely what bearer says.

Edward P'

The vicar repeated it aloud. The Queen from the gloom of her chair said: 'Let me see it.' She examined it closely but said noth-

152

ing. Skittles was breathing heavily as a result of her exertions. She had filled the wash-bowl with bloodstained clothes and as she rinsed them she hurled them out of the window. She spoke disconnectedly: 'They didn't dare put any more on paper, and there wasn't time ... There is blood on your suit, Reverend ... Is there blood on me?'

The vicar sorted out these statements. He peered at himself and thought he detected bloodstains. He dabbed at them with a wet cloth. 'Yes, you have some on you, but the stains scarcely show. What have they to say? Quickly.'

Skittles came out of the lavatory and the bedroom. 'This coach is to be lifted on to the paddle-wheel steamer *Phoebe*.'

'Yes, yes.'

'There is to be a rescue attempt at the dockside. Not shooting. Something the engineers are working on. There is a particular request to Her Majesty to be on the divan, when the time comes, firmly against the partition, and to buttress herself with pillows.'

'She is to do this now?' asked the vicar.

'Not now. No! That would give the game away. Only at the last moment.'

'The last moment will be when the coach is in the air being lowered on to the deck. What can anyone do at *that* time?'

Skittles shook her head. 'They didn't explain. They told me what to say, and I've said it.'

'And then?' pursued the vicar.

'You and me together were supposed to tie up the Nolan girl and gag her. I had a bottle of chloroform with me, from Dr Jenner. It fell on to the track.'

'You had a knife.'

'Yes, John Brown's. I might need it, he said.'

'John Brown,' repeated the Queen. No doubt it was the same knife that had been used in her service scores of times. Brown always carried a knife with him, for picnics in the mountains; he cut bread with it or slit trout and salmon caught in Balmoral streams. She found herself beginning to take a different view of Skittles. How many girls would have dared to climb aboard a doomed coach as she had done?

The train gave a jerk and seemed to be slowing down, although it had never been travelling very fast. 'Do you know where we are?' asked the vicar. Skittles pulled aside a blind and peered through the foggy night. Her knowledge of Liverpool was confined to the days when she worked in her father's skittle-alley and lived upstairs over the pub. She knew the dockside area because that was where the pub was, and on half a dozen occasions she had gone on picnic outings in the fashionable charabanc. As luck would have it, at that moment the train was edging through Seaford, one of the few outside communities she had once passed through. She recalled the names. 'We're close,' she said. 'Not more than a few minutes now.'

Some sharp raps sounded on the partition, in some code that could not be guessed at, and the three of them stared at each other, their faces drawn with concern. The vicar knew that there was nothing he could do about it; there was no Mary Nolan to respond, and it would be folly now to simulate answers. He hurried into the lavatory to inspect it. The light was bad, almost non-existent. He hurried back and searched around and under the divan. He sighed with relief when he found the reticule that had belonged to Mary Nolan. He wasted no time in hurling that out of the window.

'They'll soon be here now, ma'am,' he said to the Queen. 'If you'll permit me to do all the talking – and support me when opportunity arises . . .'

The Queen nodded a little vaguely. She had temporarily put herself in a mood, almost in a trance, where her thoughts were far away, indeed in another world altogether, with someone who was very dear to her, someone with whom she hoped soon to be reunited. Her responses tended to be automatic.

'We have to hide this young lady,' continued the vicar. 'Hide her, or get her out. They'll be watching both sides of the train now. We can't get her out. I fear disaster if they find her.' He was watching the Queen closely. 'What suggestions have you got, ma'am?'

'My bed?'

'First place they'll look.'

'Under the divan?'

'Also obvious, I fear.'

Thunderous, angry rapping now shook the partition. The Queen began to return to reality. 'I don't know where . . . There is nowhere.'

'One place,' said the vicar decisively. He looked intently at the Queen's capacious hooped skirt. Skittles was not as tiny as the Queen but she was small. If she curled herself around the Queen's feet, the skirt might conceal her. He prayed that it would. This had been a part of his plan from the beginning, the only way out of disaster that he could see.

The Queen understood; she knew what he had in mind. 'Oh God, when will this end?' she exclaimed.

The gong boomed twice, replacing the rapping.

'Get down! Hide!' hissed the vicar. Skittles ducked under the royal skirt. He made a final survey. He could see nothing wrong. 'Sit as you would normally, ma'am,' were his final instructions to the Queen. 'You may wish to read the Bible.' He composed himself as the train jerked to a stop. In the absence of Mary Nolan, he would have to open the door, and he wasted no time doing it.

Todhunter pulled himself up. In one hand he was clutching a pistol.

'Where's the girl?' were his first words.

The vicar replied mildly: 'She went into the bedroom.'

Todhunter was in there in a second; in another moment he was out again. 'What have you done with her?'

'She went in there. I saw her.'

'When?'

'Just before the train stopped.'

Todhunter addressed the Queen. 'You, ma'am, what have you to say?'

The Queen remained sitting upright, her hands clasped around the Bible on her lap. She seemed to be an expressionless spectator, as though she was not involved, much less concerned: 'She went in there. Yes.'

'When?'

'As the vicar says.'

Todhunter rapped on the partition. This was some new set of signals. Answering raps followed. He went into the lavatory, put his head through the window and began talking with his confederate. After this he left the coach. In twenty seconds McClune himself was with them. He also carried a pistol. He was much less jumpy than Todhunter, and moved quickly and with deliberation. There was no question who was the leader.

His first step was to turn up the oil-lamp. His second was to examine the divan closely. He spoke in an even, clipped voice with only a faint trace of an Irish accent: 'Where's her reticule? She had it with her.'

The vicar shook his head.

'Where did it go?' pursued McClune.

Perhaps it was a momentary mental block, but the vicar with a choice of answers preferred to be non-committal. 'I can't say.'

McClune kept at it. 'Did you see her carrying it into the bedroom, or didn't you?'

'I didn't notice,' replied the vicar awkwardly. The lie made him acutely uncomfortable even though offered in the service of his Sovereign. Almost immediately he was aware that he had made a tactical error. McClune was watching him closely. It stood to reason that, given the close physical relationship of jailor and prisoners within the confines of the train compartment, a move that any one of them might make could not escape the notice of the others. Furthermore, the vicar's voice did not carry conviction.

McClune stalked into the bedroom, turned up the second oil-lamp, and moved into the lavatory. When he emerged, he looked grim. 'Someone has broken the window-latch. Recently.' He held his right finger under the lamp. 'There are stains on the sill ... Blood, I would say ... I'll know soon ... Vicar, you're lying ... Ma'am, you're lying. What has happened to her?'

He cocked his pistol. 'She was one of us,' he said.

Whether by accident or design, the Queen with a quick sweep of her hand jerked up the window blind alongside her. The drama being played was suddenly visible to a wider audience, if anyone was watching – and they were. A picked squad of sharpshooters under the command of Lord Hartington, one of the deadliest shots in the kingdom, had been keeping pace with the royal coach on the last stage of the trip to Liverpool from Carstairs Junction. They had been travelling on the parallel line, lagging about a mile behind, but, when the royal coach was suddenly halted, the squad concealed behind the wooden walls of a flat truck had edged slowly alongside. It had been a relatively silent flanking movement, because the engine was in the rear, and the truck had the harmless appearance of part of an ordinary goods train being shunted backwards, a common sight near Carstairs.

The Queen's action took McClune by surprise. His glance was drawn through the window, and in the darkness outside he saw the grey shape of the truck, only a few feet away on the other line. A white face was peering over the side, and, by the light filtering from the compartment oil-lamp, he recognized Lord Hartington, and saw the glint of the barrel of Hartington's rifle. Although his first impulse was to execute the clergyman on the spot, he paused a moment. He lowered his pistol very slightly. In the early stages of the plot, more than a year ago, he had weighed the odds against himself, and had decided that he would be enormously lucky if he ever saw his Irish homeland again, and fantastically lucky if, somehow or other, he survived after that. One thing he was sure of : digressions could lead to disaster. The vicar was a digression. He would settle with him later. The heart of the plot centred on retaining physical control of the Queen.

McClune rapped a signal on the partition to alert Todhunter. He pulled open the coach door and made it clear that the pistol in his other hand was pointing in the direction of the Queen. He confronted Hartington, who was standing, while his half-hidden sharpshooters remained in the 'ready' position. It was the instant the vicar had been waiting for. Now that McClune's back was turned, he gave a silent signal to the Queen, the meaning of which was obvious : 'Get Skittles away !' The Queen bent down and whispered, 'Now !' Skittles uncoiled herself, rolled rapidly across the floor, and slithered into the bedroom. On the outside McClune was saying : 'You've killed or captured one of ours, and I hold the vicar responsible. I'd kill him now, but we want his story. He's going with us ... If you fire a single shot, if you get in our way, that's the end.' He slammed the door and locked it. He rapped another signal to Todhunter, listened to the answer, and seemed satisfied. The gong sounded once; the train began to move again. The fog was definitely lifting. Within minutes the train was rattling along at high speed.

McClune seated himself and examined his pistol. 'The coming stage is the vital one,' he said. 'I see no dangers myself. If your friends plan dangers, ma'am, that is up to them – and you. This coach will be lifted on to a ship. We have rehearsed it many times – in Ireland. I shall stay here, as a precaution.'

The Queen seemed to be accepting this passively until she exclaimed, 'I feel rather faint, vicar, some water please.'

The vicar hesitated. McClune nodded assent. There was a carafe near her, and the vicar filled a glass. She drank, and said : 'I must lie down.'

'Where, ma'am? The divan?' asked the vicar.

'The divan will do.'

McClune moved from his position, alert, watching. As between having the Queen on the divan or in the bedroom, he preferred the former, where she would be in view.

'Let me get a pillow,' muttered the vicar. He took one from the bedroom and put it under her head. No trace of Skittles was visible.

Silence ensued. As the train drew nearer to George's Dock, the smell of the sea coming through the ventilator was fresh and strong. The vicar was thinking deeply. 'I was too hasty with the Duke of Marlborough ... There is always a time for prayer ...'

II

The telegraphed messages, orders, and counter-orders that had passed through the hands of the Prime Minister since he had left Euston station at five in the afternoon had linked him with Liverpool, Manchester, and Scotland. All of them had a culminating point in one obscure room in Carstairs Junction, and it was not the room where the vicar was interviewed. It was a store-room.

Two of the walls were lined with shelves containing railway paraphernalia – oil, lamps, shovels, flags, drums, cases. Against a third wall was a model of the Queen's coach, in wood, done on a scale of about one inch to the foot. It was a work of art and the product of two local carpenters who were among the retainers of the Stanley family. Apart from being built to scale with respect to length, breadth, and height, it was also correct *with respect to weight and the distribution of weight*. The carpenters, Kitto and Snooks, had worked like madmen on the model. They, themselves, leaned to the finer touches that distinguish good cabinet-work, but they soon learned it was not appearance that mattered. The area of concern was weight only. At 11 p.m. the model was covered with a cloth and carried to the Prime Minister's coach on his special train.

At 11.15 p.m. the train pulled away from the junction, only three minutes ahead of the Queen's train, and eight minutes ahead of the flanking train carrying Hartington and the sharp-shooters. The mixture of lines at the junction made this possible – and to this must be added superb railway organization.

Some alterations had been made in the Prime Minister's compartment. Upholstered chairs had been removed and replaced with a batch of smaller, narrower ones, all facing in one direction. At one end of the coach the model was displayed conspicuously on a table as though on a stage, an illusion that was heightened by the activities of Kitto and Snooks, who stood to one side and were wholly absorbed in manipulating pieces of wood and string, and a number of pulleys.

At 11.30 p.m. the Prime Minister was standing in front of the model speaking to the company in front of him, the combined retinues of the Prince and the Queen, and his own.

He said : 'The Queen's coach is to be lowered by crane on to the paddle-steamer *Phoebe*. I want to emphasize the paddle-wheels. In the case of the *Phoebe* these extend at least ten feet from the hull on each side, which means that there is at least a ten-foot distance between the hull of the ship and the dock. Actually there is more: there are hempen fenders, which add another two feet. 'The width of the Queen's coach is eight feet.

'We know, further, that the coach is to be lowered into a shallow hold that has been especially built, in the rear part of the ship. Carpenters, please demonstrate ...'

The two carpenters produced a rudimentary model of a crane with pulley, and, with a simple sling attachment, hoisted up the coach. They swung it slowly in a half-circle.

'Obviously there is a second or so when the coach is over water,' continued the Prime Minister.

A voice interrupted: 'Not necessarily entirely over water, sir. If the coach swings in the air, it may be partly over the water, the dock and the ship.'

'It well may be,' the Prime Minister conceded readily, and his manner conveyed the impression that this had been anticipated. 'Sir John Cowell, your observations.'

Sir John, the only engineer present, agreed. 'That sort of motion is controlled by a man, or a couple of men, holding guide-ropes.'

'There is another point of the gravest importance,' the Prime Minister went on. 'What sort of ropes, slings, and knots are going to be used?'

This time, and without being asked, Sir John took over from the carpenters and, using the model, began showing possibilities. There were many. The demonstration was followed with such avid interest that time dissolved; it was with astonishment that the company learned they were drawing close to their destination.

Only a few hours had passed since Briggs, the former seaman, had been left near the 'Mersey Arms' by Lord Stanley. It seemed a lifetime. He had had a drink at the 'Mersey Arms', but not a second one. The place was a haunt of Irishmen. This was not unusual in an area where there were thousands of Irish, but these impressed him as being different. There was an air about them. They seemed to be waiting, and watching.

Briggs was using as his headquarters an abandoned house about a quarter of a mile from the dock. Messengers, in disguise, came and went. He himself had been reporting constantly‚ to Lord Stanley at Carstairs. But his own role now was that of a go-between. Others had moved in. Lord Stanley had used his immense influence and his circle of friends to build out of thin air an organization that in the time available could have been created in no other country but England; flexible, extemporaneous, unofficial, disciplined, and all but invisible. It was what the Prime Minister had had in mind from the beginning.

The first sign of the operation of the organization was revealed to Briggs when he was visited by a young man, who gave the name of Cutler. Later he learned it was 'Captain' Cutler. Shortly, things began to happen. Nothing that would be particularly noticed. Just occurrences. There were a number of deliveries to the rear of warehouses. Shunting-engines trundled up and down nearby spur lines. Derelicts, drunks, and women seemed to have been moved away.

Darkness helped. Even the rumours helped. They tended to explain the inexplicable. One rumour had it that a huge shipment of ammunition was expected, and unusual steps were being taken to safeguard it. Another rumour was that a foreign potentate was landing – the German Kaiser or the American President.

Getting closer to home, there was a rumour that the Queen herself had decided to come to Liverpool. Presumably to meet the potentate.

From an upper window of the abandoned house, Briggs could get a view of the River Mersey – that was before darkness fell. A warship he recognized as the *Malabar* had moved from the Birkenhead side towards the Liverpool side. It was brand new, just completed, and gleaming white. It had one funnel. Sails were furled on her three masts.

The *Phoebe* at the dockside continued to rise and fall gently. The crane had been tried out a couple of times, that is, the boom had been swung about. On the cobblestones, a pile of ropes and tackle lay ready for use.

Briggs had been receiving most urgent requests from Lord Stanley to describe this tackle, but he couldn't do it. It was too much of a jumble. He had had more luck with another urgent request – to report whether the tackle was made of chain or ropes. There were one or two naphtha flares burning near the crane, and the eerie night fog gave it the appearance of a guillotine. Voices occasionally floated across the dock as the men exchanged words with the men on the *Phoebe*.

One of his squad touched him on the shoulder. 'Train coming.' It seemed to be about a mile away and was making a dull, clattering noise. Since it was on an inside spur line, it could not be the Queen's train, which would come direct to dockside. Briggs moved to meet it. He found it halted under the lee of a warehouse shed. Doors were opening. He recognized the Prime Minister, the Prince of Wales, and the Duke of Cambridge: on various occasions he had waited at table on all of them. Lord Stanley was talking with Captain Cutler.

When Lord Stanley saw Briggs, he beckoned urgently: 'Briggs!'

'Yes, my Lord.'

'Come with me.'

He followed Lord Stanley into the train and found himself in the Prime Minister's room. At one end was a model of a coach, which he assumed to be the Queen's. Sir John Cowell was also there.

'Listen to what I am about to tell you, Briggs,' said Lord Stanley. 'Lives depend on it, including yours...'

The Queen's coach nosed its way very, very slowly on to the dock, and halted abaft the paddle-wheel of the *Phoebe* and alongside the crane.

McClune peered into the night. The view of the crane affected him in the same way that it had Briggs. The shadows cast by the flares made it look like a guillotine. Not for the first time, he shivered. Perhaps it was anticipation; it could have been fear. The disappearance of Mary Nolan had shaken him. For the last thirty minutes he had been studying the vicar, and, if he had learned anything of men during his lifetime, he felt certain that this one was incapable of murder. Capable of other things, no doubt, but not that.

Of the Queen, McClune was less sure. She could be implacable.

In time of crisis, capable of anything ... Well, there would be time during the crossing to Ireland to find out about Mary Nolan. The vicar would give in before the Queen would.

He addressed the Queen who was resting on the divan, with a rug over her and two pillows by her head (she had asked for a second); the vicar was sitting on a chair. He said : 'This is the last warning. If your friends have plans to rescue you here, dissuade them. If you wish to write a message, I'll deliver it.'

The Queen, who was staring at the ceiling, muttered, 'There will be no message.'

'Very well.' He rapped on the partition to convey a pre-arranged signal to Todhunter. He faced the vicar. 'Lie on the floor, Reverend. Face down.' The vicar dropped to the floor. He was now alongside the divan, about a foot and a half below the Queen.

McClune opened the door halfway outwards. He kept a pistol in his hand. From his position he could keep an eye on his prisoners as well as the dock without being open to direct fire.

A man left the crane and came alongside. 'Have the engine uncoupled and move away,' McClune said. Shouted orders followed. The engine moved off.

'Report on the situation,' McClune continued.

'The situation is quiet, Tim. Too quiet. We had anticipated troops by now, thousands of them. Not that they could have done a blessed thing. But where are they? I can't understand it. There's been a few people skulking around, and that's all. There's a big warship moved close in. The *Malabar*.'

'No other reports?'

'Only what you know. The trains meeting at Carstairs, and who was in 'em.'

'Did you know Mary Nolan had gone?'

'By God, no.'

'There's something afoot I can't put my hand on. I don't like the look of it. Pass the word. We must be ready ...' He pointed a finger into the darkness. 'What's that?'

Emerging was a figure who materialized as a priest; he soon reached them. He introduced himself: 'Father O'Flaherty; this is my parish.'

'My advice to you, Father, is to go away before you get hurt,' replied McClune.

'I have been hearing some confessions if you know what I mean, McClune – I take it you are McClune? It's the Church and the faith that is being hurt this day, and not me, or you. What do you think will happen when all this is over? You've heard of revenge, haven't you? If anything happens to the Queen there'll not be an Irishman in Ireland left to go to church. Madness, McClune. Wickedness, which is much worse. Will you not listen to reason?'

'Go away, Father. Go away.'

'I was terribly afraid you'd say that. Then you must listen to reason on a small matter.'

'What small matter?'

'They'll not let you move this coach from this spot in present circumstances.'

'Then the coach will be blown up ... And they know it ... And *you* may as well know it.'

'Not so fast, McClune. Not so fast. In present circumstances, I said. It's the mechanical matter of lifting the coach from dock to ship they object to. When I said a small thing, I meant it. They are not going to let the Queen be injured needlessly.'

'What do they propose?'

'An engineer to supervise the loading.'

'What engineer?'

'Cowell, or some such name. I do not know the man.'

'Is that all?'

'He would have one helper.'

'And that's the sum total of the demand?'

'That's all they told me ... except they asked for a few band instruments from the parish hall. Don't ask me why. I don't know. They're a formal people. When the Queen goes aboard ship there's always a band alongside playing patriotic music ... Well, the Queen is going aboard ... If it wasn't tragic, it would be funny ... I said to take all the instruments you want, as long as you return them.'

McClune pondered. There was logic in the first part of the

request. The band instrument part of it was inexplicable. Aloud he said : 'I like it less and less.'

'I would hope so,' was the priest's rejoinder. 'You carry a heavy burden, McClune. It will overwhelm you. And us ... It is not too late ...'

'It is too late. Go away. They can have their engineer and one helper. No one else. They'll be unarmed. In full view at all times.'

Father O'Flaherty departed. Shortly, several things happened. Captain Cutler disappeared into a warehouse which overlooked the dock, the upper windows of which were not more than thirty paces away from the *Phoebe*. He held a whispered conference with a tall figure who, when he turned round, revealed himself as Hartington. The Hartington train had arrived on yet another spur line. Surrounding him were his sharpshooters. Two more figures stalked into the group : the Prince of Wales and his friend Chaplin. The conference concluded; hampers were thrown open to disclose a cache of guns of all kinds, the finest available, from the gun-racks of Knowsley Hall.

Simultaneously, Sir John Cowell was having final words with the Prime Minister, after which he walked towards the crane accompanied by his helper, Briggs. It seemed an interminable time to them before they arrived there. They stood isolated while McClune's men sullenly uncoiled ropes. Sir John paced round the crane studying the boom, the gauges, the boiler, the drum, the brake. A colloquy took place. Briggs was seen to be demonstrating with his hands. The apparent response : resistance. Resistance gave way. Whatever the subject of the argument, changes in the hoisting preparations were under way. Two separate slings now materialized, replacing one big one. These were strung tightly around the coach, inside the front and rear wheels. Sir John and Briggs studied the whole microscopically. It received approval. Sir John gave a signal. The crane puffed. The coach was raised about a foot. It swung gently. Ropes creaked and tightened further. The coach was lowered. Guide-ropes were attached to the buffers at each end. The dress rehearsal was complete.

From some place in the darkness came sounds of music signifying a rehearsal of another kind. The music was loud and raucous and, at a guess, was supplied by the unlikely combination of drum, cymbals, cornet, and barrel-organ. An unseen orchestra was tuning up. It seemed to be under the impression that sheer noise was the end in view; and perhaps it was.

Out on the Mersey the warship *Malabar* gave a deep hoot, whether by coincidence or intent.

Sir John strode to the door of the Queen's coach, still partly open. He said to McClune, 'We're ready.'

McClune closed the door.

Sir John strode to the crane-driver. 'Follow orders exactly. ... Raise the coach slowly three feet ... Move it over the water ... Hold it there.'

The coach ascended. The men manning the guide-ropes moved with it as it swung over water. Briggs took up a position from which he could view it lengthways. He waited until the whole of the coach was over the water. Then he gave a signal. Hoisting halted.

The music was reaching a crescendo. Suddenly, Sir John removed his hat. A terrible crackling noise broke out, although partly masked by the music. A fusillade of gunfire from warehouse windows, aimed at one vital spot, snapped one of the hoisting ropes as though it were a piece of thread.

What happened next was unexpected. One end of the coach – the end with Todhunter and the gunpowder in it – now unsupported, plunged violently under water.

The Queen's section, supported by the remaining sling, remained above water, but only just, and the coach hung grotesquely in a near vertical position.

The dumbfounded crane-driver, sitting at the controls, saw and then did not see. A bullet toppled him sideways. Sir John, standing by, took over.

Then men on the dock, running for cover, were cut down by Cowell's Highlanders, who had erupted from their hiding-place, or by Hartington's sharpshooters, or by both.

Everyone on the deck of the *Phoebe* was shot down; a boarding-party swept over it.

The mathematics, the mechanics, the logistics of the operation had been brilliant ... The coach lay submerged at exactly the correct point.

The Queen, lying as she was on the divan against the partition, was the least affected by the violent upending. She simply rolled over.

The vicar, on the floor, slid under the divan and against the partition. He was a bit bruised, but really had nothing to complain about.

Skittles, under the bed in the bedroom, was affected only slightly. She was against the bedroom partition.

McClune, standing upright by the door, was hurled the length of the room and knocked senseless.

Todhunter was drowned.

With the utmost care, Sir John manoeuvred the coach out of the water. A rush of cabinet ministers, Highlanders and helpers, assisted in restoring it to equilibrium.

First into the Queen's compartment was the Duke of Cambridge, who picked up the senseless McClune and began banging him against the floor. The Prince and the Prime Minister, who were in next, stopped him. They found the Queen amazingly self-possessed. It was she who asked for assistance to get the vicar out from under the divan. The anxious Hartington lent a hand to Skittles.

'The Queen should have a drink of whisky,' prescribed Dr Jenner.

'The "Mersey Arms" is nearby,' said Lord Stanley, 'and I happen to be the landlord.'

It was a brief walk to the 'Mersey Arms'. The Queen took the Prince's arm.

The Pomp and Power of England were again assembled, this time under the happiest circumstances. The publican behind the bar was in an especially jovial mood, although his eyes were brimming with tears; and there were tears of joy and relief in other eyes too.

A sign above the door revealed the publican's name to be: John Walters. A half-opened door showed the way to a skittle-alley.

The Queen was in a strange mood. There seemed to be an impish light in her eye. She seemed to be searching the crowded room, until her gaze lighted on Skittles, dressed demurely in black. She looked angelic – at the moment.

'Bring Miss Walters to me, please,' said the Queen to Colonel Ponsonby. The Prince and Hartington, meanwhile, had wandered away and occupied a distant corner.

'Miss Walters,' said the Queen, 'I want to thank you deeply. Will you accept this little token from me?' She undid a brooch and placed it in the girl's hand.

Skittles gave a perfect curtsey. 'I really don't know what to say, ma'am ... I'll wear it everywhere.' She added, 'I'll keep it under my pillow.'

A startled look crossed the Queen's face. But she said nothing. Some things are better left unsaid.

Disraeli was extending thanks to the Reverend Mr Anderson. He spoke softly. 'If I may say so, you will be in line for preferment.'

'Thank you, sir. At times like these, one tends to speak frankly. I have to confess: I am not a believer. I am an agnostic.'

'Who *is* a believer?' enquired Disraeli, blandly. 'I doubt I believe in anything. Is *that* your only objection?'

'But the creed ...'

'Don't let us be ridiculous, Mr Anderson. But don't quote me, of course.'

The rest of the sentence was drowned by the musicians, who were now serenading the company, but in more muted tones. The company began to take it up in song ...

'The Queen, God bless her!' exclaimed the Duke of Cambridge.

'The Queen!' echoed the others, including Mr Walters behind the bar.

There was an immediate sequel to the events at Liverpool. The Prime Minister, now at Balmoral, and weary after a long trip, had fallen asleep in the anteroom. Nothing like it had happened before to the indestructible Disraeli.

Emile Dittweiler first noticed him through a crack in the door. She opened the door about six inches and told Lady Ely.

Lady Ely informed the Queen who was on her way down to dinner. The Queen peered in and smiled.

Others on the way to dinner saw him.

The Prince and the Duke of Cambridge snorted.

Grey, Ponsonby and Knollys saw him, but it was the sound of the dinner-gong that woke him with a frightful start.

At the table, the Queen smiled upon him and enquired whether he had had sweet dreams.

'No, your Majesty. A terrible nightmare.'

'Really! Can you tell us about it?'

'You were kidnapped, ma'am, and finally rescued. A long involved story.'

'Kidnapped where?'

'On Killiecrankie bridge of all places.'

'How amusing.'

Despite himself, Disraeli shuddered. The dream had had a mad logic to it. It could all be possible. Except, perhaps, the gong.

It was by far the most vivid and detailed dream he had ever had. Deeply disturbing.

Epilogue

The famous (or infamous) Hastings-Chaplin *cause célèbre* is, of course, a fact of history, and those interested can pursue it in detail in *The Pocket Venus*, by Henry Blyth, published by Walker & Co, New York, 1966; or in the much earlier *Henry Chaplin*, a biographical memoir by his daughter, the Marchioness of Londonderry, published by Macmillan & Co, London, 1926, which, however, presents an understandably one-sided point of view.

The Reverend Charles Anderson was an eccentric clergyman, 1826–1893, who was vicar of St John's, Limehouse. In the 1890s he visited his friend, Edward Clodd, and said to him: 'I have given up all belief in the Creeds and, as far as agnosticism can be defined, I am an agnostic. I have only my income of £300 a year and, being a single man without any claims on me, I spend more than two-thirds of it on the upkeep of the church, payment of the choir, and the rest of it. That leaves me £2 a week to live on, which I manage to do; so if I chuck the thing I am penniless; it will be a case of standing on the kerb outside your bank with matches and bootlaces for sale. Now I ask you as an old friend what shall I do?'

'Clodd's answer was: 'Stick to your job. I know what a lot of good work you are doing down there.'

A brief biographical note on Anderson appears in *Memories* by Edward Clodd, published by Watts & Co, London, 1926, and the above quotation is used by permission. Anderson actually was a member of the Curates' Clerical Club, known as the CCC, and he was an admirer of both T. H. Huxley and Samuel Butler. It is a measure of Anderson's mind that to him was due the first publication of Samuel Butler's *Psalm of Montreal*, in the *Spectator*, 18 May 1878.

The most lovable character in the case of characters in *The Day They Kidnapped Queen Victoria* is Henry Ponsonby, Equerry but later Private Secretary to Queen Victoria. Truly 'A Man for all Seasons', as is revealed by the compelling book, written by his son, Arthur Ponsonby – *Henry Ponsonby, Queen Victoria's Private Secretary: His Life from His Letters* (Macmillan, London, 1942). Among his attributes was a delightful sense of humour.

'Skittles' Walters was a very real person indeed. She was the subject of a violent editorial onslaught by the *Daily Telegraph* in the 1860s – and would the Queen have taken pleasure in that! She enjoyed an annuity from Hartington for more than half a century. She was tiny, graceful, an interminable talker who swore violently. According to reports she was interested in modern art and serious reading. Presumably, 'modern art' in the 1860s meant the pre-Raphaelites.

She was probably the most influential English courtesan of her time. She was also a first-class horsewoman.

Sir Edwin Landseer apparently did paint Skittles. He was a remarkable imitator of animal and bird calls. At one period of his life he suffered an emotional breakdown.

Acknowledgements

The remarks of Joe, the coachman, concerning rats are taken verbatim from a salty character named Jimmy Shaw, proprietor of a London sporting pub, who is quoted in Mayhew's celebrated *London Labour and the London Poor*, first published in 1851.